The *Essence* of Pandemonium

E. M. Tremiti

PublishAmerica
Baltimore

First printing

ISBN: 1-59129-348-0
PUBLISHED BY PUBLISHAMERICA
BOOK PUBLISHERS
www.publishamerica.com
Baltimore

Printed in the United States of America

To my Grandpas,
who didn't get the chance to read this book

I love you both.

To the Gargers',
I really hope you all
enjoy this story as much as
I loved writing it! It's
great to have you as neighbours!
E.M. Tremiti

Acknowledgments

There are many people who have helped me through the years and deserve to be thanked. My fourth grade teacher, Mr. Kelly Cooke, for opening my eyes to the wondrous world of writing, and to all the teachers who offered their help and time to me. A special thank you to my Dad and Mom for giving so much effort into letting this dream come true. To my brother, Paul, for helping me with the technical stuff, and a very big THANKS to a friend who gave her time at a last minute notice: thank you, Suzanne. To all my friends and family and everyone else out there: I hope you like this book.

The darkness comes filling in
Like a wave of panic and regrets
The inky sadness engulfs the empty space
Like a wonderful memory of a lie
A soft swelling touches the truth
Like an unwanted storm
The unwelcome depression slips overhead
Like a morning chased away by incensed raindrops
Then you must escape
Like a wild wind trying to capture you
It seems impossible....

Chapter 1

Prolog

Heather Learl had slipped into a subconscious world of delicate dreams. She fantasized about all the ice cream she would devour and the huge array of presents she would receive the next day at her birthday party. Heather was to be six on the following morning and it seemed like such a big age. Her mind depicted images of attending school for a full day and taking the school bus that all the other children on her street rode. She was terribly excited. Heather dreamed about all the pictures she would paint and all the drawings she would draw. Her mind raced excitedly and refused to lay in quiet as her imagination concocted an exceedingly impressive list of reasons why turning six was going to be absolutely spellbinding.

Suddenly, her visions of happiness disappeared and rotated into abnormal, frightening illusions. Colors blurred together in twisted patterns, and she found herself standing in the middle of an enormous forest. Heather stood staring at a girl she swore she knew, but she was so much older. Realizing that she and the girl were teenagers sent chills hurtling through her body. Unable to file through her mind and depict who was standing across from her, Heather suddenly remembered that there was no time to think. There was something chasing them and they had to run rapidly away from it. Pushing her way through the thick air, Heather could not control the sensation that she couldn't breathe in, and her aching limbs felt like weighted sandbags dragging her to the carpeted floor.

The other girl was shouting, "Run faster, Heather! We have to run faster!"

Heather wished to answer, but she was too winded. The fact that she had to keep running cleared her mind of all other obstacles. With sweat pouring over her face, she pressed on, and then, without thinking, she tripped. The girl looked down at her, screaming for her to get up. It was so hard to move, her eyes filled with tears, but she had to keep fighting, for Jane's sake. The name struck Heather like a bolt of lightning; the girl yelling at her was her close friend Jane. That moment's hesitation let their oppressor close in, and the creature was all around them. Heather could feel it squeezing them, but what was it? It was massive, and yet her eyes couldn't see it.

It was about to turn so Heather could see its face when, "Chirp! Chirp! Chirp!"

Heather, still lying down, glanced at her window. She had forgotten to shut it and now there were tons of chirping noises cascading through her window like a waterfall. The air smelled fresh and cool; the sky was only a medium blue like that of a sea or ocean. There were only a few clouds, long and wispy; they gave off a sense of tranquility on the soft, early spring morning. She looked at her digital clock; it read 5:43 a.m. Heather sat upright in her bed and felt sweat drip down her back. Her hair was in knots and tangled up in more places than one. Her light pink bed sheets were half hanging off the bed as if she had been tossing and turning all night.

Heather hopped down from the top of her bunk bed. She landed with a thump on the floor. No one slept on the bottom bunk, but she had always preferred the top. Walking groggily over to her window, she noticed a chilly breeze flow past her. It felt too cold for this time of year, and Heather quickly shut her window. The sound of chirping was now very distant and faint. She climbed back up into her bed, pulled the sheets up to her chin and closed her eyes.

Maybe if she had been older she would have remembered the dream in the far-off years to come, but as she was already too excited about her birthday and school, the dream quickly slipped into a place at the back of her mind where it would remain, forever.

I'll try my best to relate this to you. It all happened when I made a mistake. I wasn't supposed to care but somehow it, well... it didn't turn out like that. I know that you don't understand but I don't feel any other way to explain. It all just got so out of control....

Chapter 2

11 years later

Highflying birds flew through the air as clouds scudded across the brightening sky. The long-awaited end of winter was near and the last of the snow had melted. Trees donned small buds, which were growing rapidly on every branch. The bushes surrounding a small, quaint home were beginning to grow bright luscious berries. The little house stood amid many trees that gently laid gray patterns on the richly-colored green grass. Blue shutters stood out from the house's white background and the many windows overlooked the oncoming beauty of the seasons, though the occupants inside were completely unaware of the outside attractions.

"Mark, turn on the TV," mumbled Mark McTerm's twin sister as she slumped down the stairs toward the kitchen. Being twins, they both had light brown hair and dull green eyes. Mark owned plain and quiet qualities, while Jane was energetic and constantly moving. She always had a way of making her dull eyes sparkle with an unnoticed brilliance.

"Mark," Jane repeated, getting annoyed.

"Okay, okay."

Click.

"Oh," Jane yawned, "it's just the news...change the channel."

"Wait a second, I like the news."

"Fine," Jane answered as she sat down on a wooden chair and rested her head on the kitchen table.

"Welcome back to the New Jersey six o'clock news," the newscaster announced. "We have just received the startling and tragic word that Myrtle McTerm, the wealthy resident of upper New York, has been proclaimed dead. To make matters worse, the cause of death is still unknown...."

"Mark, did you just hear that?" Jane jerked herself up so fast that a bolt of pain came shooting through her head.

"Yeah, I, I think so."

"But, wouldn't...?" Jane paused, a look of disbelief written on her face. Keeping her eyes glued to the TV, she yelled in a quivering voice, "Mom! Mom, something's happened to Aunt Myrt!"

Myrtle McTerm was always by herself and hardly seen at any social events. A rather cold person is what many people thought of her. She was known all over New York for one simple reason: she was rich. Due to luck and a few wealthy husbands Myrtle was going to live out her days as an affluent woman. Her mansion was located in upper New York where she lived with her two kids. The children and her brother were the only family she had, but she only visited the McTerm family about once every five years.

"Mom, Mom!" Jane yelled as she raced up her stairs, a little unsure of how to feel or act.

Once they entered their parents' room, Jane and Mark found their mother, Cathy McTerm, sitting on the corner of her bed, sobbing softly.

"Mom, are you all right?"

"I have something very upsetting to tell you."

"Well, don't bother, we just heard about it on the news," Mark said regretfully with a tinge of blame in his voice.

"Oh, you poor children. Your father is very upset too; his sister was always so kind."

Jane shot a sideways glance at Mark but didn't say anything.

"What should we do? This is just so sudden, I don't know what to say or think or..." Jane's voice trailed off.

"Do you know why she died, Mom?" Mark asked shyly.

"No, we were called this morning by the hospital and they informed us only that she had passed away. The nurse wasn't very helpful. Your father is at the hospital right now trying to sort things out."

"What are we supposed to do?" Jane repeated.

"Why don't you try to make it through school? If you want to come home, I'll be here."

They continued the conversation a few more minutes before running outside to catch the school bus.

At the high school, Heather was looking out the window at the same sky she saw every day. Being a calm, deep-thinking person, her voice was clear but often silent. Heather, Jane, Mark, and the other seniors were having lunch. Jane was sitting beside Heather watching her other friends converse with each other. She was usually very talkative, but today Jane sat still, staring at them blankly. Her eyes rolled over the faces of her friends and she began to name them absentmindedly.

"Tonya Fredrick, Carrie Thompson, Colleen Swenson, Kristie Peterson, Tara Dawn, Marybeth..."

"Jane?" Heather said softly while nudging her.

Jane averted her eyes from her friends and stared at the ceiling.

"Dismissed," a lunch lady said as she patted Jane's lunch table. Everyone rose and left. Jane entered her next class, history, and sat down slowly.

"Hello, class, would you please excuse me for a moment? I would like to talk to Jane first."

Jane stepped outside into the hallway and looked up at her teacher.

"I already know..." Jane began but her teacher interrupted her.

"I didn't want to be the one to tell you this, but since it's already getting around school, I would rather have you hear it from me." He took a deep breath. "It has been decided that your Aunt did not die a natural death, she, she, ah, she was murdered."

Jane went completely blank like she couldn't believe what she had just heard. A blinding light seemed to fill her eyes, and a panic rose abruptly in her heart. Moments later, the voice of her friend Tara brought her back to reality.

"Jane, Jane, are you all right?" Tara said as she ran out of the classroom concerned.

"What?" Jane said softly, not really talking to anyone.

"Stop staring at me like that," Tara replied sharply.

Jane started to sob. "Oh, this is horrible. Why can't I wake up?"

"Clam down Jane, please," said Heather, who also had been in that class and had just left to join them.

Heather's brown hair brushed Tara's shoulder as she bent down to get eye to eye with Jane. Her chocolate eyes seemed to swirl around her long eyelashes. Heather met Jane's pale emerald eyes, and Jane quickly looked away.

"No! No! I won't clam down, and I'm not okay!" And with that Jane ran down the stairs and around the hall, sitting down against the lockers once she was out of sight.

Sobbing, Jane tried to calm down. "I don't want to believe it. Who would do anything like that? No, I can't believe it." At first Jane decided that she wished to go home, but as she began to walk back toward her classroom, she wondered if her mom knew. If she didn't, there was no way Jane wanted to tell her. Realizing that the bell had just rung, Jane turned and began to walk up the stairs, disbelief playing on her face. "Why can't I wake up?" she repeated to herself.

As Jane turned a corner she almost bumped into Whitney R., Whitney B., Heather, Diana, and Lindsey. A dirty blonde with hazel eyes, Diana was a long-time friend to Jane. They'd been friends since the second grade. Lindsey had just moved to New Jersey about three years before but immediately found a friend with Jane. Whitney R. and Whitney B. were almost always together. They had matching brown hair but Whitney R. owned brisk baby-blue eyes that matched her impulsive attitude. They all stopped short and stared at Jane with anxious expressions.

Jane looked at them with big watery eyes.

"Hi," said Lindsey, her light blonde hair laying against her bright blue eyes. " I mean...I don't know what to say, Jane. Math is next if you've decided to stay."

"We don't want to miss that, right, Jane?" Whitney B. asked sarcastically.

Jane smiled through her tears. "Right."

After Jane's smile disappeared, she returned to her sad and lonely trance.

"Oh," Jane said wearily, "Why her? What did she do?"

"I feel so awful for you, Jane. You can go home if you need to," Whitney R. stated.

"Yeah, she's right, Jane. Bye, guys, see you later. Meet me at my locker before we go home," Heather said. She was the only one who didn't have math class as seventh period, out of the five of them.

"Bye," replied Lindsey as they entered Mrs. Meyers' classroom.

Everyone stared at them when they entered. "Oh no, we're late," whispered Diana.

"Just what I need," Jane whispered back.

"Ladies," said Mrs. Meyers, "I think you have some explaining to do."

Just then the small phone on the classroom wall started to ring. Mrs. Meyers picked it up and began talking softly, "Yes.... sure."

"Jane, you're wanted in the office with your things, and Lindsey, the principal would like to see you at the end of the period."

She turned to the remaining three girls. "Now, what was I saying?"

Lindsey took this opportunity wisely, "You were just telling us to sit down."

"Of course I was, now take a seat and not another word from any of you."

"Yes, Mrs. Meyers," they replied in unison as they sat down in their seats.

Jane had just finished collecting her things from her locker and was walking down the hallway to the office when her brother Mike ran up to her.

"Why are you here?" Jane asked.

"I have no idea," he replied. "They picked me up from school

15

and wouldn't tell me without you and Mark." Mike was only twelve and was enrolled in the nearby middle school. His features were nothing like Jane's or Mark's. His hair was fluffy and resembled the color of a brand-new fire engine. His red hair matched his complexion, which consisted of thousands of tiny freckles. Finished off with a medium build and a rambunctious attitude, Mike was definitely the troublemaker of the family.

They walked down the hall together until they arrived at the office. Before entering, Jane flashed a brief smile at a girl that stood by the office doors. Her light caramel-colored hair fell down to her chin and her eyes smiled brightly back. Her cheeks each owned one thin stripe of light brown freckles that looked nothing like Mike's. She opened the door for Jane and Mike as she waited for her own parents. Jane put her things on the floor and asked what was going on.

The lady at the desk replied, "You will have to quiet down; the principal is on the phone in the next room."

"Sorry," Jane McTerm whispered as she peered into the room that was attached to the office and saw the principal sitting at his desk holding a phone lightly in his hand. She couldn't make out what he was saying, but she guessed that it had something to do with Lindsey and her overzealous attitude that always seemed to get her into trouble. Jane looked out the window as one of her friends walked by. A moment later she entered.

"Hi, Courtney," Jane whispered.

Courtney smiled back as she picked up one of the spring softball flyers that had been available in the office. Then waved goodbye as she exited.

"Oh, and Mrs...McTerm," the lady at the desk said as she looked at the school sign-out sheet, "You'll have to sign Mark out on a separate line."

"Of course," replied Mrs. McTerm as she reached for the clipboard.

Mrs. McTerm's husband, Jake McTerm, was there too. He had dirty blond hair and was about five foot ten; though Mark was already taller than him, Jake never admitted to it.

"I think we better tell the kids outside, Cathy," Mr. McTerm said. "Oh, I'm sure you could stay inside," the lady at the desk replied, but it didn't matter anyway because they had already grabbed their belongings and were headed out the door.

Jane and Mark walked in silence with curiosity eating away at them. They came to a halt once they reached their parents' mini-van. The color of the car was a cherry red, something like a shiny plum. The nine-year-old car had a few dented spots from a couple of skateboards and baseballs, but it was the only car Jane or Mark ever got to drive.

"Have you heard about Aunt Myrt?" Jake said as he fought back a tear in the corner of his eye. One by one, Jane, Mark and Mike all nodded.

"Well, I know how upsetting this is, and I didn't think that now would be a good time to tell you this, but your mom thought otherwise. See, you guys have heard everything from people other than us, and we just wanted to make things clear this time." Jake took a deep breath. "Aunt Myrtle had two houses, the smaller one that she had been currently staying in and the huge one in upstate New York. I never knew of this until know but...."

"What, Dad?" Mike said softly.

Mrs. McTerm was trying to stay quiet, but she saw the worried look in Jane's eyes and couldn't hold them in suspense any longer. "Even though this wasn't a natural death," Mrs. McTerm cut in, "well, we, ah, what your father is trying to say is your aunt left us her mansion and almost all of her wealth. The police are saying that she was robbed and that her money may have been the, um, motive. What she still has now is left to your father and a smaller portion to her children."

"Are you serious?" Mike asked slowly.

Jake just nodded.

It was a moment Jane would not be able to describe. Her heart felt badly for her aunt, but her head filled shock wondering what this would mean for her family. She had never thought about what would happen if her aunt died, and she never had even considered what would happen if her aunt was murdered. Jane shivered. Her eyes showed neither emotions of sadness or happiness. They just stared with a barren emotion at the sky.

It started.

Chapter 3

The sun flew through the trees and wove in between the clouds as Mr. McTerm drove home. Jane had rolled her window down and now a pleasant breeze flowed past her. She breathed it in gratefully. The coolness of it tried to calm her nerves, but a steady swelling of unexplainable feelings refused to be subdued. As they drove into the driveway none of them spoke.

Jake looked to each of his children before he began, "I know that all of you have many questions. I would like to have the funeral before we talk too much about what has been left to us. All I will say for right now is that we will not be moving into any of your aunt's mansions. The larger one was left to your cousins anyway. Even the smaller one would be much too large for us, but we won't be selling it either. The house that we live in now is too small; Mike and Mark are sharing a room. I think that we will be moving, just not there. Also, I would like to add that spending a profuse amount of her money does not agree with me, so we will be saving as much as possible."

They sat in silence for a minute, then Mike spoke up and asked the question they all were thinking. "How much money did she leave us?"

"We'll discuss it later."

"Dad," Jane asked, "I'll still go to the same school, right? We're not going to move out of New Jersey, are we?"

"Of course not, nothing like that will change," he answered.

A pale light covered the land and the sun refused to show. In its place were small droplets of rain and a howling wind. The morning had started out almost bright and sunny. Everyone who claimed to know Myrtle McTerm showed to the funeral. As morning turned to early evening, dark clouds had descended over the sky. Many said their prayers and left, but Jane and her family, along with other close kin, stayed. The conditions worsened, and finally Jake gave the final word. "We all knew this sad day had to come. Although none of us expected it so soon. We will never forget her or the way she talked and smiled. As we go home tonight we'll wonder how we will ever get used to life like this, but as time goes on we'll realize that she was a great person who would want us to live happily." Jake closed his eyes and let the rain hit him freely, then like the rest of them, he turned and left.

"Thanks for coming," Jane whispered to Heather.

"I would've come anyway, even if you hadn't asked me." Heather paused. "All those flowers look so pretty. I know that your aunt will be very pleased with all those wonderful red roses."

Jane glanced sideways at Heather and smiled. "Heather, is this the kind of funeral you'd want?"

Heather stopped walking and looked at Jane, "What an odd question. I guess, I mean, as long as all my friends and family came." She breathed in. "And if I got all different kinds of flowers like purple, red, and yellow."

"Personally, I think I'd prefer white roses," Jane replied.

"Hey, Jane, who are those two kids?" Heather said, pointing to two infants.

"They're my cousins. They spent a lot of there time with my aunt; I don't think they ever see their father. Some are even saying that they were there when it happened." Jane's voice weakened.

Within a week Mr. and Mrs. McTerm had picked out a huge house when compared to their tiny home that was for sale. They hadn't shown Jane, Mark or Mike yet because they had requested it be their decision. It then took them another week and a half to get packed, and finally they were in their mini-van driving to their new home with the moving truck not far behind.

As they turned onto a road with a meadow on their right and a small forest on their left, a loud noise issued from behind them. The mini-van went to a halt and so did the moving truck. Mr. McTerm stepped out of his car to see what was the matter.

He asked the moving men to explain why they heard that loud crash. "Well, you see," explained the moving men, "the back of the moving truck was closed incorrectly and something fell out. I think it was that big lamp." He tried to avoid Jake's stare.

"It wasn't tied right and must of fallen out, ain't that right?" the moving man asked his partner.

"Yep," his partner replied.

"I thought you two were professionals?" inquired Jake.

"Umm, the guys that normally work this truck let us take it because we had to destroy some stuff."

"What does that mean?" Mr. McTerm eyed them suspiciously.

The other moving man stepped in front of his partner and hastily replied, "Nothin'. It don't mean nothin'. We are movin' men with a different truck than we're used to, that's all." He pulled his hat farther down his forehead.

After staring at them for a minute, Jake sighed, "I guess all save you two...gentlemen the trouble and get it myself. Wouldn't want the two of you to break it on your way back!" Jake motioned for Mark to come and help.

"Coming, Dad." Mark swung the car door open and ran over to where his dad was standing. "What do you want?"

"I need you to help me go and get that lamp." He pointed to the lamp. It was partly covered by the underbrush of the forest.

"Shouldn't they be getting it for you? It was their fault," said Mark as he pointed to the two moving men. They were fighting about something and tried not to make eye contact with Jake or Mark.

Jake replied, "We can do it. I don't trust them."

"Fine," Mark said as he followed his dad down a small hill. They had to walk through the thick trees to get to the lamp.

"Perfect!" Jake said angrily as he looked down at the lamp. Besides it being filthy, it had a long crack running down the side of it.

"On three, lift," Jake said to Mark.

"No way! I'm not touching that!" Mark stepped away in disgust.

"Get over here and left on three. Sometimes I think you're worse then your sister."

Insulted, Mark stepped over to the lamp and waited for his dad to say three.

They picked up the lamp only to realize that is was much heavier then they had thought.

They were almost at the edge of the forest when Mark twisted his ankle in a narrow ditch and fell to the ground with a thud.

"Are you okay?" asked Jake, concerned.

"Oh, I'm fine, I guess," said Mark as Jake helped him up. "Hey, what's this?" Mark held up a picture of two toddlers. Suddenly, Mark recognized the children. "It's a picture of Aunt Myrt's kids. It wasn't taken very long ago because of the date that's printed on it."

"Let me see that," Mr. McTerm said to Mark. Mark handed over the picture to him, who studied it carefully. "You're right, it most certainly is them. You should give this to Jane; she would appreciate it more than you. We have plenty pictures of the toddlers, but I'm sure Jane will want it."

As Jake handed the picture back to Mark, he glanced at it one last time. "Maybe it just fell out of the truck and the wind blew it."

"Yeah, I don't remember it though," Mark answered. He put the picture in his pocket and added, "Let's get this thing back to the moving van." They both looked down at the lamp.

At last they were ready to leave and Mark handed the picture to Jane. "Here, we found this on the way back to the car."

"Why would you find it in the middle of those trees?" Jane asked as she sat looking at the picture. She had recognized the two toddlers instantly.

"Must have fallen out of the truck along with the lamp."

"But the pictures are in boxes. How could it fall out?" Jane asked, not satisfied with Mark's answer.

"Just luck I guess," Mark added nonchalantly.

Look at a picture, then turn it around and upside-down. See the view that lies hidden in shadows, the side that no one noticed, and the little mark in the corner that changes everything.

Chapter 4

A cool spring morning, a peaceful sky and still clouds added a relaxing mood that hung about the air, and it left the day undisturbed and looking rather ordinary. A large office building sat on the corner of a crowded street. Busy traffic drove by the building unaware of any events taking place inside.

Walking into the building, a person in a navy suit looked straight ahead. Two staircases and one elevator on his left were the only ways up. In front of him stood a large, glamorous marble staircase. Next to the elevator was the other staircase. It was narrow with a glass door in front of it and had been covered with a light carpet. He walked up to the large marble staircase, then, as if reconsidering, turned and walked to the nearest elevator. Stepping inside, he pressed the button for the middle floor. Once the doors reopened he stepped out onto the tenth floor. At that moment, he turned left and walked around the corner of the hallway into a small office.

"Sorry I'm late."

"Don't even try it. Where were you?" a tall man in a pitch-black suit snapped as he stood up from the desk he'd been sitting behind.

"Nowhere. The cab got stuck in traffic," this man, not quite as tall as the other but sturdily built with light brown hair, replied harshly.

"Then you walk. I saw you walk around the corner of that street to get here!"

"Oh, so now you're following me!"

"Should I?!"

For a moment they just stood there staring blankly at each other, hot anger rising in each of them. The strain of everything was playing them both, catching them and taking away the concentration they need.

"Stop it. Can't you see you two aren't solvin' anything by bickerin'?"

"Don't even start with me," the man in the black suit said, staring at the third figure in the room who had been unnoticed until he spoke.

"You can't expect me to be in here on the minute. I've got to make this meeting not happen, so sometimes it takes more time than expected."

"I'm sick of your damn alibis. No one will care if you take a twenty-minute break. They won't even take note of it."

"You're way too risky."

"Do you have it?" the other man spoke up again, anxious to get this over with.

"Yeah, I got it and I intend on keeping it that way," he said as he pulled an object from his navy coat pocket.

"What's that supposed to mean?" the tallest man questioned.

"That means that I'm not handing it over to you, so don't ask."

"Let's see it."

The man opened a hard, thin box carefully and pulled out a picture with negatives.

"You did it," the quietest of the three spoke up in awe.

"Not personally, but here it is."

"Let me hold it. Just to make sure you're not pulling any tricks," the man with the black suit said, missing the quick glance that passed between the other two.

"I guess you could hold it. I understand your wanting to check it out."

"You act as if it's a toy," the man in the black suit snickered as he took the picture out of the box. He flipped it around and inspected both sides. He looked up, satisfied. "Good job. Here, take it."

The man in the navy suit held the box out instead of his hand. "Just take it, what's your problem?"

As he eyed him suspiciously, the third man stepped out of the shadows again and said rather abruptly, "Wait, I want to hold it."

"Fine, clam down," the man with the navy suit said as he glared at him.

Looking slightly unsure, the tallest one looked from one to the other. At last, he handed the picture to the one who had spoken up.

"Ah," the man with the navy suit said casually as he looked at his watch, "your alibi ends in five minutes."

"Mine?" the man with the black suit said with a sigh.

"Yep."

"Why do these little tricks of yours have to end at different times?"

"They are not tricks; without them we'd all be under suspicion. Anyway, they end at different times so we don't get linked together. I thought you'd be smart enough to figure that out."

Offended, the man in the black suit picked up his coat and left, eyeing the other two before leaving the room.

As soon as he left, the man in the navy suit gave the other man a swift blow to his head.

He cried out painfully, "I know, I know, I almost blew it! But I didn't, he bought it."

The man in the navy suit clamped a hand over his mouth. "Sssshhhh. He could still be out there. I can't believe I have to deal with you." Releasing his hand, he crept to the door, opened it slightly, and peered outside.

"Sorry," the smaller man mumbled.

"He's not there." The taller man seemed relieved. He stood up straight and added, "What was with your, 'You did it!' line? I told you to act as if you hadn't seen the picture before, not like it was the most amazing thing your dim-witted eyes had ever seen!"

Ignoring his statement, the smaller, stockier man asked, "What do we do now?"

"First of all, we go over the plan again."

"Why? I know it by heart."

"Because I want it beaten through that thick skull of yours so no more slip-ups happen like the one today!"

"I would hardly call it a slip-up."

"Well, I would, so start talking."

The smaller man took a deep breath, leaned against the wall half-covered by shadows and began to speak. "First, we needed a careful plan; then, we needed the right tools. The camera was important; next, you sent me and some guy, who, by the way, was a pain to deal with, to destroy the original pic..."

"Skip over the part we've already done," the tall man said in an exasperated voice. "Wait, by the way, how did that go?"

The smaller man stood silently as if holding something back.

"You did it, right?"

"Of course, yeah, everythin' is fine. I did it just like you were askin' me to."

"Fine, continue."

"Right. We have very legitimate suspicions that our partner is going to take our share for himself, so now we have the new change of plans. Instead of handin' in an innocent man, we're gonna hand in one that's already guilty." The smaller man smiled as he quoted the man in the navy suit's words.

"Keep going."

"We got the finger prints and..."

"You are wearing gloves, right?" For a moment the man in the navy suit felt a wave of panic, but that all subdued when the smaller man held out his gloved hands with the picture.

"Here, I'll save you the breath of askin' for it." The smaller man put the picture back in the box; the other man just nodded.

The conversation continued for another five minutes. Then the man in the navy suit left the same way he had come in, while the smaller man sat down at his desk.

He tucked the picture back into his navy suit as he pushed open the doors and stepped out into the cool sunshine, letting the glass doors that read "Lawyers and Associates" swing loosely behind him.

Back in the office, the smallest man pulled the shades up and turned the rest of his lights on. As soon as he sat down, the phone rang.

"Hello?"

"Hello, I'm calling about the case that's scheduled to begin. Are you ready to present your evidence?" a female voice questioned.

"Actually, it's being brought over right now."

"That means you still think you have a suspect?"

"Just wait, I'm sure we've got the right man."

"Okay. I'll be waiting. Are you bringing it over?"

"No, my partner is. He should be there in a matter of minutes."

"Bye, then."

"Bye."

He sat back in his chair and took in a deep breath. Rubbing his head, he reached into his desk for an Advil. Noticing his hand shaking slightly, he pressed his other hand on top of it. "You're fine," he said sternly to himself. "You've been under more pressure than this, now calm down." Trying to relax, he stood up and left his office for a drink of water.

Jane had returned to school with a clouded mind. Everyone around her passed by as if they didn't know what to say. Jane tried to enjoy herself, but that sickening feeling that her new home came from the death of her aunt just couldn't settle inside her. She knew that even her friends were wondering how much money had been left to her family, but her parents just wouldn't tell. All they said was, "Be thankful for our new house." And Jane was.

It was the end of the school day when Heather walked up to her.

"Are you doing anything this afternoon?" Heather asked.

"No, just staying home. Unless my parents have something planned."

Jane could tell that Heather wanted to come and see her new home.

"Heather, why don't you come over today? I'll show you around my new house."

"I'd love to," Heather said as she turned to leave.

Jane slipped her backpack onto her shoulders and started walking toward the school doors. She was late getting to her locker so there was hardly anyone left in the hallways. As she passed by a classroom, something caught her eye. It was a picture that took up the entire blackboard. The picture was of some kind of hideous animal. It looked like a snake but there was something different about it—its size. It looked enormous; its dark eyes seemed to be looking straight into Jane's. Its long, thick black coils sickened her. She took a step back from the window she'd been looking through and studied the picture. It scared her even though it was just a picture, a drawing. Looking at the bottom of the poster, she read its name, "Anaconda. Found in Brazil. Can be fifteen to forty-five feet in length." Jane shivered; there was something about it that touched an uneasy feeling inside her.

"Most kids don't like to stick around here," a teacher yelled from down the hall.

Jane looked back at her, falsely smiled and left. She had just made it onto her bus before they started pulling out. She wished that she could drive home with her own car.

"Maybe now I can," Jane said to herself, very excited at the idea. With the new money they had come into, maybe her parents would buy her a new car. Then she scolded herself sternly for trying to profit from all this.

The bus ride home was much more enjoyable than the one to school. Jane looked out the bus window at the far-off hills and beautiful countryside. At every house they passed, there were tons of flowers, big and bright. White or light brown picket fences at almost every home and big yards with fresh cut grass, oaks, evergreens, and beach trees. This route was much different from her old one with small rundown yards and homes. The sun was out and there wasn't a cloud in the sky. Birds hummed their high-pitched songs while the bees flew in eager patterns. Spring was coming in full bloom.

The bus came to Jane's stop and she got off with Mark. Quickly,

Jane pulled her sleeves as far down her arms as she could, since she had no coat.

Turning to Mark, she voiced her thoughts. "It's really windy. It was so mild earlier, I wish it still was."

"It's fine out. I'm just glad the snows melted," Mark answered quietly.

Jane looked in front of her and was happy to see her new home loom into view. Walking silently the rest of the way, she began to feel that welling inside her, that excited feeling that she tried to hide.

Helping someone at another's expense didn't seem so wrong to me, not yet.

Chapter 5

The house had four floors, including the finished basement. On the first floor there was the living room, dining room, kitchen and two extra rooms. On the second floor were Mike's room, Mr. and Mrs. McTerm's room, the family room, a bonus room and one guest room. Finally, there was the top floor. It would have been considered an attic if it hadn't been so large and already finished. It held Jane's room, Mark's room and a computer room. Jane marveled at how spacious it was. She was used to a cluttered, older, cozy-type home. Nothing like this had ever crossed her mind. She ran around the side of her house as she heard her parents' voices. Running up to them, she stopped and dropped her backpack onto the ground.

"Mom."

"Yes, Jane."

"Can Heather come over so I can show her the new house?"

"We were planning a surprise for you."

"What do you mean?"

"Remember how your father always wanted horses and a farm?"

"Yeah," Jane replied. She remembered. When Jane was only five her dad almost bought a farm instead of a house when they first moved to New Jersey, but it ended up being an improbable idea.

"Well, now that we can afford it, he bought two horses. They have to stay in a stable that's only a five-minute walk from here. I didn't know this until after we bought the house, but we have a trail in our backyard. It can be used to go horseback riding on; if you and Heather want, you can go ride."

"Really?" Jane was completely taken by surprise. She had gone horseback riding many times in the past. Whenever they went to see family on vacations, they always found time for the sport.

Mr. McTerm sat up straight in his lawn chair. "You have to be careful, Jane. If Heather doesn't want to, don't force her. And, ah, one more thing, we have decided not to spend any more on us. You know what I mean. Your mother and I feel that we have a comfortable home and something we've always wanted. That's what Aunt Myrt always wished we had. What I'm trying to say is, we're going to save the rest of the money and not spend it carelessly."

"Okay, okay. I'll go call her." Very excitedly, Jane ran into her new house.

After a few minutes she came back out and started walking down the road. As she was about to disappear from view, Mike came running up from behind her.

"Where are you going?"

"I'm going to get Heather and go horseback riding. Hey, why are you home so early?" Jane asked, puzzled. The middle school didn't get out for one more hour.

"I got a fever," Mike replied happily.

"Sure," Jane said, eyeing him. Mike was into jokes and schemes, and she knew that he just didn't want to go to school.

"Mom told me about the horses. Pretty neat, huh?"

"I can't quite believe it."

"I might go riding later on tonight."

"No, I don't think you will. You'll be too busy resting. Now go back inside before you get even sicker." Jane stood and watched her brother walk slowly back to the house. Smiling, she turned around and pressed on. She was going to stop at Heather's house and they would walk to the stable together.

Jane started humming as Heather's small but well-kept house

appeared from around the bend.

The pretty, petite house had a light blue color covering it. It donned white shutters and beautiful landscaping. Jane smelled the fresh air. Spring smelled so good to her. She looked up at the sky; the sun would not begin to set for another few hours.

Jane skipped up the walkway and rang the doorbell.

Heather's mom answered it. "Hello. Oh, Jane, hi! How are you! Won't you come in?"

Jane would have suspected that Heather's mom was trying to act exceedingly nice to her if she wasn't accustomed to the constant pampering she always provided.

Jane stepped into the house while the brown-haired, blue-eyed mother walked up the steps to go find Heather.

Jane gazed around the short hallway that led to the kitchen and stairs. Golden brown chairs, table and a matching counter made the room give off a very welcome appearance. There were many different signs in the kitchen that read messages like, "home sweet home" and "home is where your heart is." Jane loved the small house. It was nice and comfortable, but now that she had a big, spacious house, it seemed a little different. She didn't like the new feeling; she had known this house forever.

Jane turned her head as Heather ran down the stairs, skipping the last three.

"Hi Jane," she said, almost out of breath.

"Hi. Do you like horseback riding?" Jane asked kind of suddenly.

"Me?" Heather paused, then smiled. "How would I know? I've never done it before."

Jane looked at her. "Really?"

Heather just nodded her head.

Jane opened the door and they both stepped outside.

"Would you like to try it?"

They continued the conversation as they stood in front of Heather's house. Once Heather had all the information, she went back inside to talk to her mom. A few moments later she emerged.

"Okay, I'll go."

It took about ten minutes to walk to the stable from Heather's house.

All Jane had to do was show an ID and they were in. Heather was extremely nervous but excited. They climbed onto the horses and started very slowly down a path, reaching Jane's property rather quickly. The beginning of the ride was very nerve-racking for Heather. She continuously asked questions and kept her arms very stiff, but after fifteen minutes she began to relax. Jane could tell that she was really enjoying the ride.

The sky was beginning to turn to a light purple. It looked as though if Jane touched it, it would feel like soft velvet. It was then when Jane suggested that they turn around and head back to the stable.

"Jane why don't we go down to that stream first? It will give us more room to turn around."

"Sure."

"Hey, Jane, I'll race you."

At first Jane looked reluctant.

"I don't mean really fast, just like a jog. We were going that fast before."

"All right, Heather, I'll race you. Wait till I say three. Okay?"

Heather nodded.

"One..." Jane paused. "Three!"

Jane's horse started running down the trail with Heather not that far behind, yelling, "No fair! You cheater! I can hear you laughing, Ja...ahhhhh!"

By the time Jane stopped, she had already reached the stream. At first she thought Heather was still behind her, but when she turned around, she saw Heather's horse laying down on the ground, trying feverishly to stand up.

Jumping off her horse, Jane tied the reins to a tree and ran over to Heather. "Heather, Heather what's wrong?"

Tears were streaming down her face. "Jane I, I fell; the horse must have tripped on something."

Jane looked over Heather's shoulder and saw a thick fungus-covered root sticking out of the ground. The dark green fern and fungus crawled over the roots and up the tree that it belonged to. Jane stared at it for a moment. She didn't remember seeing it before. She would have pointed it out to Heather, but it was too late now.

Jane looked back at Heather and stated, "Heather, your horse is standing up and looks fine. Let me tie him to a tree, then I'll help you."

As fast as she could, Jane tied the horse to a tree branch and knelt down beside Heather.

"Ohhhh, my arm and my ankle; my ankle hurts the worst!"

Jane looked at Heather's shoulder. It had a scratch on it and was trickling blood down her arm onto her plain green sweater.

Jane thought to herself, "What can I do? I have to get help."

She was about to suggest the idea when Heather started complaining again.

"Don't look at my arm, look at my ankle. Do something, Jane!"

"Okay, Heather, just stay calm. I'm going to go back to my house to get a parent or someone that can help you. It's not that far; I should be back in about thirty minutes."

Jane had turned to leave when Heather started to shout, "No, Jane! Don't leave me here. There might be wild animals walking around in these woods! Please don't leave me here!" Heather's voice was starting to sound desperate.

"Well, what can I do, Heather?" Jane asked.

"I have an idea."

"Fine. Just hurry up and tell me before it gets dark," Jane replied.

"All right, this is what we'll do...."

In about five minutes, Jane was on her horse with Heather sitting behind her. The other horse was behind them as Heather held onto its reins.

The sky was turning an ever-so-fading color purple, which was turning darker and darker by the minute. There was a gentle wind causing a faint rustle among the treetops. Owls were just beginning to make loud hooting noises when Jane and Heather arrived back at Jane's house.

Jane started ringing the doorbell feverishly.

Mr. McTerm opened the door. "Jane, where have you been? Dinner's been ready."

Jane didn't answer. She just led her dad to where Heather had successfully climbed off the horse.

"Heather, what happened to you?" Mr. McTerm asked, seeing the blood on her sweater.

"The horse tripped over a root. My ankle hurts; I need to sit down."

"Right. Let's get you inside straightaway," Mr. McTerm said.

They brought Heather to their living room. Heather gazed around at the furniture and the prettiest fireplace she had seen in her life. Made with real marble and pieces of sliver, it gave off a glamorous look. The ceiling was at least twenty feet high, and cream-colored paint covered each wall.

"Here, Heather, sit here," Jane said as Heather snapped back into reality.

Jane was arranging pillows on a section of the sandy-colored couch so Heather could sit down and rest her leg on a glass table that was placed a few feet away.

Mr. McTerm had left the room to get ice, and Mrs. McTerm went to call Mrs. Learl.

Jane sat down next to Heather and said apologetically, "Heather, I'm sorry."

"Sorry? Sorry for what?"

"Sorry for letting you ride that horse when you had never even gone horseback riding before."

"Oh, come on, Jane! I had a great time, and it couldn't have been your fault because that root was there! I can't wait to go horseback riding again. I'll just have to be more careful."

"Do you think you broke it?" Jane said, eyeing Heather's ankle.

"I don't think so." Heather smiled. "When you break something it's not supposed to hurt this much."

Within another fifteen minutes, Mr. McTerm brought the ice in and Jane heard the doorbell ring.

She rose and said as she left the room, "Heather, I'll be right back. I'm just going to find out if that's your mom." And with that, she left the room.

Once Jane had left, Heather began to think, "When Jane had started to walk back to her house to go and get help, something happened to me." She whispered to herself, "I started to panic, and then when I closed my eyes I saw this blank blackness. Like you always see, but there was something so fearful about it. I...I don't get it." Heather decided that she was just scared and put it into the back of her mind.

Jane was also pondering over Heather's insistence on panicking like that as she walked to the front door. "She must have just been afraid. I probably would have been if it was me," Jane thought. "But it *wasn't* me."

Jane was about to answer the door when she saw her mom already had. Mrs. Learl stood in the doorway, concerned.

"Jane, go tell Heather that her mom will be there in a minute," Mrs. McTerm said softly.

When Jane returned to where Heather was still sitting, she sat down next to her, "Your mom's coming."

"Jane, I don't want you to feel bad."

"I still do, but I have something to ask you. Why did you get so scared back there? I know I would be, but you once camped out in that very same woods with nothing but a blanket." Jane grinned at Heather.

"I was ten and it was the middle of summer." Heather laughed. "I know this must sound odd, but I really don't know."

Before they could add to the conversation, Mrs. Learl and Mrs. McTerm entered the room.

"Are you okay, Heather?"

"I did something to my ankle, and I have a bad scratch on my shoulder."

"We have to get you home immediately."

Once they had gone, Jane asked her mom what time it was.

Mrs. McTerm looked at her old and worn leather watch. "It's 9:17, Jane. Why do you ask?"

Jane swallowed. "Because the trial for Aunt Myrt starts at 9:30."

She paused. "On channel four." Jane was surprised that the trial would be televised, but it had blown up. She was sure that it was part the money, part the mysterious evidence, and, of course, part the murder.

It was a hard subject to talk about in Jane's house. The whole McTerm family had been informed that they had a suspect. Mr. McTerm had made the decision to not attend the hearings unless they were asked to.

"I guess we can watch it. I just don't know how to handle all this. Just thinking of any person...." Mrs. McTerm stopped herself and headed for the family room.

A flower cannot cast its own shadow on a bright sunny day.
Something else is always there.

Chapter 6

Maribell entered the room clothed in black pants, a black blouse and an apron. "Dinner is ready, Mrs. McTerm."

"Maribell?"

"Yes."

"Would you mind if you set up dinner in the family room today instead of the dinning room?"

"Sure, right away. Give me, ah, let's say ten minutes?"

"That's fine."

Maribell was the McTerms' maid. Even when they lived in their old home she came about once a week, and now almost every day. Maribell came from Peru; she had dark hair that hung somewhere between her chin and shoulders. Overall, she was a very pleasant lady. Mrs. McTerm turned to Jane after Maribell had left. "Jane, I have something to ask you. I've been trying to block out the trial and the publicity, but I need to know what happened. I don't really know anything about the trial, and if you wouldn't mind, could you just tell me what you know?"

Jane looked slightly over her mom's shoulder. It was impossible for Jane to look her mom in the eye when talking about this. Sighing softly, she told all she knew. "Barry Lonad called Dad just about an hour ago. He's a detective on the case. Dad said that the suspect is a man that worked on finances, some type of lawyer. He helped Aunt Myrt with her bills and stuff. His name is Sam, Sam something, and the reason they suspect him now is a mistake on his part. It was said that the very day of the incident, he was over at the house taking pictures of Aunt Myrt and her two kids. Aunt Myrt wanted them for something. He came back later that night and Aunt Myrt's kids...kind of ran into him. They were supposed to be in bed. He needed an excuse for being there so they wouldn't run and tell their mom. He then took the same camera he'd been using that day and told them he needed some more photos. Furthermore, he took a picture of them and that was that. Aunt Myrt placed a 911 call at 12:46 and the picture he had taken had a date and time on it. The date was the same and the time was 12:43. I'm not sure how they found the picture, but they did and it even has his finger prints on it."

"How did it have the date and time on it?" Mrs. McTerm asked slowly.

"Mom, our video camera does that; it just shows up in the corner of the screen."

"Why was he there in the first place?"

"He stole an awful lot of her money and belongings. No one has found the money or property yet."

"Really?" her mom asked quietly.

They stood there unsure of what to do. Jane's explanation made her heart depressed, and she felt this emptiness inside her. It all sounded so simple, but it wasn't the lonely death of someone, it was murder.

"Let's go into the family room now." Mrs. McTerm tried to sound effortless, but what Jane had said left small tears in the corner of her eyes.

When they entered the family room, they noticed that their old TV trays had been placed in front of their brown leather couch. Mr. McTerm sat in an old velvet chair that was over-stuffed with goose feathers. It was one of the few things he refused to give up. The old chair was eminently comfortable and gave off a lazy mood, a lazy mood that vanished at this moment.

Whenever Maribell stayed and cooked dinner, it was always something unique. There was a leek and onion soup that had been put in small bowls at the edge of there plates. A bigger bowl was placed on the right side of their TV trays and had been filled with dried fruit mixed in with nuts. On the middle of their plate was a small fried chicken and mashed potatoes with gravy. On a separate small plate was a bowl of homemade pudding with whipped cream.

Mrs. McTerm complimented Maribell on the food as she exited the room while Mike tried not to show his disgust.

"What kind of soup is this?" he said, pushing it away.

Mrs. McTerm just commented quietly that she might have some of his if he just left it on the edge of his tray.

They all just sat there for a minute, and then right as Mark reached for his food, he remembered that it was his turn to say grace. After taking a deep breath he began,

"Graciously we thank you lord for the food we eat

On all the seasons we think of you

During everything we see and do."

Mark said that every time it was his turn. Being a very simplistic person, he liked to stick to simple things.

Mike switched on the TV and they sat and watched. Jane, sitting down, took a pecan from the dish of nuts and threw it at Mike. It bounced off his forehead and landed on the carpeted floor.

"Hey!" Mike said as he angrily picked up a handful of nuts and threw them at Jane. She ducked and they hit Mark instead. Jane just giggled as she forgot the purpose of them sitting in the family room. As Jane's eyes turned back toward the TV, her heart sank and she turned quiet.

"You know what," Mr. McTerm spoke up suddenly, "I don't think we should watch this. Let's just eat in peace."

Jane, Mike and Mark looked at Mrs. McTerm for that to be confirmed.

"You three, just go somewhere else if you really want to watch it," Mrs. McTerm said as she turned off the TV.

"Okay," Jane replied as she walked toward the door. "Ouch!"

Jane spun around to find Mike trying to hide a smile and a nut lying by her shoes.

"You know that hit my head!" Jane said, annoyed.

"That's it! Everybody out, Jane, Mark and Mike! Go and find something to do," Mrs. McTerm said in a no-nonsense tone.

"But I'm not done eating yet!" Mike replied.

Once they had left with the exception of Mike, Mr. McTerm began to speak. "What are we going to do with them? I wish they were more like Mark."

"No you don't. Mark hasn't been perfect all his life," Mrs. McTerm replied as she took a sip of her coffee. "Do you remember when Jane was fourteen...no wait, fifteen and came home from Lindsey's party?"

"Oh, I remember," Jake said as a slight smile spread across his face.

Mike sat quietly as curiosity masked his features.

"Anyway, she had come home two hours later then she was supposed to and the next morning was a school day. I asked Mark to make sure that Jane woke up and got ready in time for school." She stopped, trying to keep herself from laughing out loud. "The next thing I hear is a scream; I run upstairs and find that Mark had taken a bucket of ice cold water and thrown it on her! That definitely woke her up! I swear not one day has passed since Jane hasn't locked her door when she goes to bed."

Mike stood up to leave. "Sounds like fun."

"Not for Jane," Mrs. McTerm responded as he walked out the door.

"Oh, right," Mike said as he closed it behind him.

Jane's room was much more spacious than her old one. She had light yellow walls and her three windows had mellow green and yellow stripes on them. About a year ago she had dismissed all her old furniture and instead bought what she had always wanted: a soft, fuzzy couch. Her bed was placed at the far end of her room, next to a small round table that had been painted a light green to match Jane's walls. Her white phone had been placed on top of it. Jane's

TV was pressed against the middle of her left wall, right in front of the fuzzy couch.

Jane had sat down on her couch, picked up her remote and turned to channel four when she heard someone knocking at her door.

"What is it? I'm trying to watch the trial. I've missed enough of it already."

"Can we come in and watch it with you?" The voice could be none other than Mrs. McTerm's.

"One second." Jane regretfully rose from her cozy position and unlocked her door. In came Mike, Mark and Mrs. McTerm.

Jane turned up the volume and sat down on her couch. The only sound that was audible other than what was issuing from the TV was the cling of Mike's spoon as he scraped a pure white bowl, trying to get every speck of ice cream out of it. Jane ignored the noise and concentrated on the TV.

Finally, the judge took his seat. He cut a curious figure. His hair was completely white and he looked to be in his late sixties. Having his dark brown eyes stand out from his white hair gave him a very intelligent look. His thick, black, square eyeglasses made him appear stern, and when he began to speak, his voice was hard and cold. He spoke in a clear, concise tone: "Ladies and gentlemen of the jury, I have a murder case to present to you today. Just a month ago a robbery and murder took place at a mansion not far from here. Myrtle McTerm was the victim. Two point eight million dollars were stolen, which includes the estimated price of her stolen belongings. The suspect is Sam Norman..."

I knew I had gone too far. When you do something you know you can't take back, you never think you did the wrong thing. Everything is under control....because it has to be.

Chapter 7

The clock on Heather's nightstand ticked to a steady pace, breaking the otherwise silent air. She had fallen into a deep, unconscious sleep. Her mom had arranged for Heather to have her ankle examined by her doctor the following morning. Heather lay in an intensely uncomfortable position since she couldn't put pressure on her ankle. The night droned on with Heather oblivious to it.

There was something about the woods that she had rode in with Jane that afternoon. It brought back a memory so faint that it made no sense. As she slept, all that she saw was green, faint colors and sounds too far off to understand. There was an uncanny feel to the surroundings, but the only thing that she could see clearly was fear. It was almost spelled out on the faded canopy of colors. Heather found herself standing in the middle of green, dark green and light green mixing with a haunting black, and sounds, so many far-off sounds. What were they saying? Heather began to get hauntingly frustrated.

"We have to make it back!"

"Who was saying that?" Heather thought to herself. Suddenly, she collapsed and the sounds grew fainter. Then she saw something coming at her from behind a blotch of swirling colors. As it moved behind the colors, they rippled like a stone thrown at a pond. Heather had nowhere to run; the colors engulfed her and she could see the colors moving closer toward her. They were coming for her, going faster and faster. "Ahhhhaaaaa!" Heather screamed aloud as she sat upright in her bed.

"Oh my gosh! Heather, please. You scared me half to death. Are you okay? I was just trying to wake you; you have to get ready for your doctor appointment. I'm sorry."

"No, Mom. It wasn't you, just a bad dream."

"What about?"

"Funny, I can't remember. Oh well, who wants to remember a nightmare in the first place?"

"As long as you're all right. We have to leave in a half an hour," Heather's mom said in a cheery voice. Before she left, she took one last glance at Heather. She was sitting on her bed, softly talking to herself.

Jane woke up two hours earlier then Heather because she had forgotten to turn off her alarm clock. Unable to go back to sleep, she rolled out of bed and paced around her room, when she heard someone knocking none too gently on her door.

"What do you want?" Jane asked angrily.

The voice could be none other then Mike's. "Are you awake? It's Saturday. I heard your alarm clock go off. That was pretty stupid of you."

"Yes, I'm awake. Or even if I wasn't I definitely would be now." Jane yawned. "I'm trying to wake up, but I'm just so tired. I can't get myself back to sleep either."

Jane walked over to her door, yawned once more, then opened it. "Now Mike, I want you to tell me what you want and go away...ahhhhaaaaa! I'm going to kill you! You better run!" Jane yelled in a shrill voice full of rage as she half-tripped over the now-empty bucket that Mike dropped as he turned and fled.

Mark's room was next door to Jane's, so he woke up as soon as he heard Jane scream. Running out of his room, he followed Jane, trying to find out what was going on. Mr. and Mrs. McTerm ran out of their room and onto the main staircase when their eyes came into contact with the scene below: Mike running in the lead, laughing hysterically; Jane hard on his heels shrieking; and Mark running behind Jane, yelling, "What is going on? Jane, why are you soaking wet?"

At first Mr. and Mrs. McTerm were dumbfounded, but as Mr. McTerm picked up the empty bucket with small droplets of water still in it, he looked up at his wife. "You don't think?"

"He wouldn't, not so soon."

Jake nodded his head.

They ran over to Jane, trying to hold her away from Mike. At that point Mike had collapsed onto the tiled floor, completely exhaled but still laughing uncontrollably.

"What is going on? Mike, what did you do?" Mark asked, still puzzled at what had occurred.

"You are in a lot of trouble, Mike," Mrs. McTerm said sternly, still clutching Jane's arm.

Mike could barely answer, "D, don't blame me completely. Jane, you sh, should see yourself now, hahahaha. Mark was a bad influence, hahaha."

"What are you taking about?" Mark asked.

"If you hadn't d, don, hahaha, done this to Jane before I, I would never have gotten the idea, so, so there!"

"Oh Mike, you didn't dump a bucket of water on Jane, did you?" Mark said in a sort of disappointed voice.

"Yes, I did."

"But that was my..." Mark didn't have time to finish because Jane interrupted him.

"How could you do this? I don't care whose idea it was! I am soaking wet! I'll get you back, just wait! You won't know when, but I won't forget!" And with that, an infuriated Jane marched up the stairs to her room and slammed the door.

"Mike, we will talk about this later," Mr. McTerm muttered, trying to hide his smile.

"I can't get a punishment that was worse than Mark got!" Mike yelled as he ran up the stairs.

As soon as he left, Mr. and Mrs. McTerm began shaking with mirth.

"Leave it to the kids to cheer us up," Mr. McTerm said.

"It's so good that they are still them, you know what I mean?"

"Yeah, Mike still steals my ideas and copies me!" Mark yelled back as he bounded up the stairs to his room.

By the time Jane had showered and changed, it was about the time when Heather had woken up. Jane was about to call her when she thought twice about the idea. "Heather will need her rest; I'll call her in a few days," Jane whispered to herself as she dialed the phone numbered of another close friend.

After the telephone rang a few times a weary and exhausted voice answered, "Hello."

"Hi, is Diana there?"

"One moment please."

"Diana! Phone!"

Jane winced, pulling the phone away from her ear.

"I'm coming! You don't have to yell!"

A few seconds later, the voice of Diana could be heard through the telephone, "Hi. Who is it?"

"It's Jane."

"Oh, hi, Jane! Don't mind my sister; she's just tired. Her friend was driving her home from the mall and the car broke down; to make a long story short, she didn't get home until quarter to four."

"In the morning?"

"Yep."

"I was wondering if you could come over to my house today."

"Hold on."

"Mom....Mom!"

"What is it, Diana?"

"Can I go over to..."

"Yes, yes you can. Be back at six; if they invite you to have dinner, then give me a call," her mother answered.

"I can come over. I'll walk. It's not that far, and it's nice and cool this morning."

"Okay, see you later."

"Hey, maybe we can do something on Monday too."

"Isn't Monday a school day?"

"It would be if spring vacation hadn't started."

"Spring vacation starts today?"

"I thought you knew."

"Oh yeah, now I remember."

"Okay, well, bye."

"Bye."

Jane set the phone back on its receiver, smiling softly to herself. She liked Diana's family; they were so blunt and simple. In her large household Diana had two sisters, ages sixteen and three, and four brothers, ages six, twelve, fourteen, and twenty-two. Her oldest brother still lived at home and worked to help support the family.

Jane combed her hair and looked in her full-length mirror. She was wearing a new pair of jean shorts and a light blue tank top that matched her freshly painted toes. Slipping on her sandals, she ran out her door and down the steps to the kitchen for breakfast.

Mrs. McTerm entered the kitchen, turned the sink on to wash her hands and began to converse with Jane. "I have good and bad news; which do you want first?"

"Umm, bad."

"I was on the phone with Heather's mom, and she said that the doctor found out that Heather has a third-degree sprained ankle."

"Really? How long will it take to heal?"

"I'm not sure. Mrs. Learl said that she would be off her crutches in about two to three weeks."

"Should I call her and ask her how she's feeling?"

"Mrs. Learl said that she will be resting today, so why don't you give her a call tomorrow?"

"Sure, and the good news?"

"Mike is grounded for two weeks."

"Only two? That's not good news."

"It's good enough," Mrs. McTerm answered.

"Fine, Diana should be here soon," Jane said as she crammed the last bite of her waffle into her mouth. Standing up, she handed her plate to her mom and ran out the door.

Jane stepped outside on her front steps and waited for Diana to arrive. She gazed around at her home. "I wish Aunt Myrt could see it." Jane felt a sickness creep into her stomach and sat down. Closing her eyes, she breathed in the cool air. It smelled so sweet and pleasant. Jane still felt strange whenever she entered her new home, like she didn't belong there.

"Hi!"

"Oh," Jane looked up, "Hi, Diana, I didn't even see you coming."

"It's kind of hard to see things with your eyes shut."

"Yeah, I guess so." Jane smiled.

Diana looked at Jane and voiced, "What do you want to do?"

"Come in. I'll show you my room."

"Great, I've been wanting to see it."

As they started walking through the hallways and stairs that led to Jane's room, you could almost see the awe on Diana's face. She stared at the wallpaper and the floors that either were wood, carpet, rug or tile. Most windows donned the same curtains that were in Jane's old home, but they looked different in this new setting. Entering Jane's room, Diana looked out her window. To her surprise, dark clouds had began to cover the light blue sky, and it gave off the appearance that it was going to rain.

Heather stared out her car window as her mom drove her home from the doctor's office. The clouds had already covered the sky where they were, and now little droplets of water began to hit the car windows. Heather turned her head so she could gaze out the back window and watch the patterns of each droplet.

Her mom glanced back at her. As she focused her eyes back on the road, she started talking to Heather, "Heather dear, stop turning your neck like that. It'll get sore. I have a question to ask you."

"What, Mother?" Heather replied, turning her head toward her mom.

"You've been acting kind of strange today. You seem very distant; is there something wrong?"

"No, nothing's wrong." Heather paused. "But something's been bothering me."

"What?"

"You know why my ankle is sprained, right?"

"Yes, because you were going horseback riding and your horse tripped."

"But when Jane started to run back and get help, I started to see something in my mind, and I started to hear sounds that I hadn't heard before. I felt so terrified that I yelled for Jane to come back."

"Honey, maybe you where just scared of being left alone in the woods," her mom replied as she made a left turn.

"That's it. But not these woods, other woods."

"Explain," her mom said in a confused voice.

"I felt scared because I knew there was something in a forest that I'm afraid of, but somehow I knew it wasn't these woods. I wanted the images in my mind and the sounds to go away, but they wouldn't, so I called for Jane to come back. This never happened to me before."

"You've never been horseback riding before."

"Mom, that's not why this happened."

"Why then?"

"I don't know. Do you have any idea?"

"You're probably just scared from a past experience of being in the woods and being somewhere that's like the place where it happened..."

"Or would happen."

"I'm not following."

"Maybe it's some image to warn me."

" Maybe you've watched too many movies."

"Mom, that is such a cliché. Right, don't believe me."

"All right," Mrs. Learl answered as she pulled into their driveway.

"Here, let me help you with that," she said as she opened the door for Heather and helped pull out her crutches.

"I'm taking a nap as soon as we get inside," Mrs. Learl announced.

"Me too. There's not much else to do."

The rain pounded the ground with an unrelenting force while a thick gray mist covered the air. Clouds made the sky disappear and everything donned a bleak appearance.

Once they were inside and dried off, Heather limped to her sofa and lay down. Pulling a homemade quilt up to her chin, she closed her eyes. It wasn't long before a heavy weight pulled her eyelids shut and sleep overtook her.

Heather looked around; she saw nothing familiar.

"You're dreaming again," she said to herself. "This is just another nightmare. You'll wake up soon."

"No, you won't. This is your reality; you will never wake up again."

"What's that suppose to mean?" Heather said, trying to pass off a tough attitude.

The voice was old and dull. It suspended over her and she heard it from all angles. There was no escaping it, and the fog that lay by her feet echoed the voice's every syllable. It sent wild chills flying down Heather's back.

"Sanity's worst nightmare is the thought of an unrelenting insanity that approaches one and eventually steals one away. So, try to understand while you still can," the voice said calmly.

"This isn't real! Heather, please wake up soon."

"Taking to yourself? That is odd."

"No, this dream is odd." Heather stared at her surroundings. Nothing had a definite shape. Black, green and splotches of shaded white stood in unidentified shapes all around her. Heather was becoming severely frustrated. "What is it? Do you want something from me?"

"I thought you didn't care! I thought you were just dreaming!" the voice cracked.

"I am!"

The voice began to sing in a soft whisper that lurked beneath every shadow,

"Some have been told

As this story will unfold
Made from crooks
Your friends will suffer
But you already know this
From no other."

After the voice had repeated itself several times, Heather finally interrupted, "Why are you singing? What does it mean? I want to wake up!"

"But you can't dear, but you can't." The voice faded and all grew quiet.

"Dear, dear, wake up," Heather's mom said as she shook Heather gently.

"What, what?" Heather's eyes flashed open. "Mom, I had a dream."

"That's fairly normal," Mrs. Learl replied, smiling.

"I can't remember it, either."

"How do you know you had one, then?"

"It was more of a nightmare," Heather said to herself.

"Heather, look at me. How do you know that you had a nightmare?"

"I just do, well, I can remember part of it. Hand me that pencil and a piece of paper."

Mrs. Learl turned around, picked up the objects and handed them to Heather.

"Wait a second." After scribbling something down on the paper, she looked up at her mom. Handing the piece of paper over to her, she asked, "Have you heard this before?"

Skimming the paragraph, Mrs. Learl replied, "Never in my whole life have I heard those words in that order. Just because you heard them in a dream doesn't mean it's magic, if that's what you're thinking. Get up and come to the kitchen. It's time for dinner."

Dinner had just been finished at the McTerm house. Having a maid prepare food for them was one of the few things that didn't take too long to get used to. Jane never really cared about meal times.

She would have a bite here or buy a hamburger from some fast food place on her way home from summer jobs. Now missing a meal was like missing a chance to go out to eat. Not that her mom wasn't a good cook, but this was Maribell's job.

Diana had stayed for dinner and was in Jane's room waiting for her to bring up some popcorn to eat while they watched the next day of the court case.

"Open the door! Open the door!"

"I'm coming Jane, clam down," Diana replied as she hurried to the door and took one of the bowls of popcorn that Jane had been juggling from her.

Jane grew quiet as she saw her TV.

"Jane?"

"Last night my family and I drove to my aunt's grave and laid flowers for her," Jane voiced.

"Really?"

"Yeah, it's so hard to think about her, but I didn't know her that well. I hadn't seen her for years. That just makes things worse, because now I can never see her again."

"I'm sorry, Jane," Diana replied, looking at Jane's eyes.

After a moment's silence Jane said, "Let's sit down."

They each took a seat, and Jane switched on the TV, put it on the right channel, sat back and waited.

Finally, after the commercials, the court commenced.

As the judge began to speak, the little talking that was audible vanished. "As you already know, we have found a motive for this crime." He paused. "The defendants have been asking questions as to why this picture is so important. Well, the picture was taken only three minutes before the 911 call was made by Myrtle McTerm. Meaning that whoever took the picture must have been there when the murder took place. The picture has been entered as exhibit A. We have found the finger prints of Sam Norman on it, and so far he has no alibi."

Only the two lawyers sitting on the prosecution side noticed the suspect flinch at the judge's remark. He flashed a glance toward them, and they quickly turned and faced front.

"I think he did it. Why must people like that be so stupid to leave evidence behind with their fingerprints on it?" Diana stated.

"It doesn't seem right to me. I mean why *would* he leave a picture behind?"

"He didn't mean to Jane."

"Yeah, but why would he do that?"

"He took enough stuff to make him rich."

"And how did he get it all out of the house without any help?"

Diana was about to answer when she stopped and turned back toward the TV. "I don't know Jane, must have been pretty hard."

Jane turned her head away from Diana and faced the TV. They were showing a close-up of the picture before the commercial break. A sudden shock burst through Jane's heart as it skipped a beat. A tickling of disbelief ran down her spine. "Déjà vu," she whispered.

"What?"

"See that picture on the TV?"

"Yeah."

Jane looked pale and rather uncertain, but she jumped up out of the couch and turned toward one wall. Pointing to the picture Mark had found, she added, "That's the same picture I have." Her mouth moved slowly, almost not willing to say it.

"Just look at it and tell me it's not," Jane said almost shoving the frame in Diana's face.

Diana took the picture in her hands and quickly tossed it onto the other side of the couch.

"Why'd you do that?" Jane snapped.

"That's it. But how?"

Before they could add to the conversation, Mrs. McTerm yelled from downstairs, "Diana, your mom's here!"

"I'm coming!" Diana yelled back. "What are you going to do?" she replied as she left Jane's room.

"I don't know," Jane answered as she stared at the picture at the opposite end of her couch. A sudden chill entered the room, and

Jane felt a nervousness creep up behind her. She felt compelled to thrown the picture out, crush it or even destroy it.

Trying to calm down, Jane set the picture back and decided to leave the issue until tomorrow. She looked at her clock; it read 11:03 p.m. Jane yawned. The picture gave her uncanny feelings in the pit of her stomach. Jane walked outside her room to her bathroom, which was across the hall. Jane smiled as she looked at herself in the mirror and thought, "I'm so glad I have my own bathroom." She remembered when she lived in her other house, and they all had to fight over one solitary bathroom.

After brushing her teeth and combing her hair, she put on her pajamas and slipped into bed. Turning off the light, she whispered to herself, "There was something peculiar about the picture I saw on TV. It looked different, but I don't know how. It was the same but not quite." Right as she dozed off, it hit her like a ton of bricks.

When a problem spirals out, certain things are always blamed on others. Never can anyone say that it was all his or her fault. Nothing is all one someone's fault. It wasn't my entire fault. I didn't do everything. I won't take responsibility for this...

Chapter 8

Jane woke up early the next morning, and to her disappointment, dark somber clouds had covered the sky again and raindrops pounded the ground mercilessly.

Putting on a news channel, Jane sat down glumly on her couch. Her mood quickly changed when she heard one of the newscasters mention yesterday's court case.

The newscaster began her report, "In light of yesterday's court case, Sam Norman is now the number one suspect. We were not allowed to photograph the evidence, but we have a detailed drawing of the picture that has proven he was in the house the same time of the murder." She paused as the drawing appeared on the screen. "Now, here's Jack with weather."

Click.

Jane tried to close the awful feelings inside her. She tried not to think about what must have happened. It was too much. There was something pulling inside her that knew she couldn't sit and hide. Picking up her phone, she decided to call Barry Lonad. Barry Lonad was a policeman and a detective presently working on the case. He had become somewhat of a friend to Mr. McTerm, and Jane knew of no one else to call.

"Hello."

"Hi, is Barry Lonad there?"

"Where did you get this number, miss?" the pleasant female voice said slowly.

"I am a relative of Myrtle McTerm; Mr. Lonad gave my family this number."

"Oh, hold on please." The lady sounded apologetic.

Jane felt slightly uncomfortable but sat patiently until he picked up the phone.

"Hello, this is Barry Lonad." His voice was gruff and stern.

"This is Jane McTerm, Jake McTerm's daughter."

There was silence on the other end.

"I have something important to tell you."

Finally, he spoke again, "Jane? Jane, yes, I've met you before. If it's important, I'll listen."

"Okay." Jane took a deep breath. "I was watching the court case yesterday and saw the picture that was turned in as evidence. At first I didn't think anything of it, but then I realized that the picture was exactly like the one my brother found out in a forest. We were moving to our new house and he found it on the side of the road. We all thought it had fallen out of the moving truck, but I swear it's the same one."

At first all Jane heard was silence. She held her breath waiting for him to speak.

Barry cleared his throat before answering, "This is extremely unbelievable. You're sure that this is the same picture?"

"Yes."

"The exact same photograph?"

Jane swallowed and added, "One thing is different."

"And what's that?"

"This is the same picture, but the date on the bottom isn't the same."

Silence, but this time it was an eerie silence; before it was just a half-paying-attention silence.

"Are you trying to play a joke on me or something like that?"

Jane was taken aback. Quickly she answered, "No, of course not. I'm telling the truth."

"Jane, I want you to go put your mom or dad on the phone."

"Hold on," Jane replied. She rushed out of her bedroom door, down the stairs, into her kitchen and to her frustration her mom wasn't there. Maribell approached her. "What are you looking for, dear?"

"Do you know where my mom is?"

"I do actually. She and your dad are taking your brother, Mike, to the doctor."

"Both of them?"

"Yes, they left about ten minutes ago."

"But why? Mike doesn't need both parents to...."

"Clam down, Janet...

"It's Jane."

"Oh, sorry. Jane, what do you need?"

"Nothing." Jane turned around and left the kitchen. "I hope he hasn't hung up," Jane mumbled to herself as she entered her room.

"Hello."

"Hello. Is your mom or dad there?" Barry repeated.

"No. They're not here."

"Oh, okay. Just listen carefully."

"All right."

"I really don't want to send myself or someone else down to get the picture. I would hate to cause more publicity to your family. So you can either send it in or bring it down yourself."

"I would bring it down."

"I meant your mom or dad."

"I could, though; I'm seventeen."

"Just listen to this and tell your parents. This court is taking place in New York, just forty-five minutes from where you live. You could easily make a day trip and drive up here, but make sure it's wrapped up carefully in a package. When you reach the courthouse, there will be lots of security. Show them the package and they will deliver it to one of the labs.

"What if they don't believe me?" Jane asked.

"I will call them ahead of time to make sure that they know you're coming."

"You really think this is easier than having someone come and pick it up?"

"It's not so much the easy part or the publicity part." He paused. "If for some reason the picture is different or a fake, we don't want it to get out. It could blow up and could even become serious."

"What you're saying is, the best way to get this picture to you is by bringing it to the courthouse?"

"I would think so."

"I guess I can get it to the courthouse. I'll need good directions."

"Your dad went to the courthouse once when I met with him. He can drive it down. I know that your parents aren't home, but if he has forgotten where it is, tell him it would probably be on a map."

After Jane had finished talking to Barry, she looked down at her phone and then at the picture that was still in its glass frame. She knew that Barry didn't really believe her story. He seemed interested, maybe even baffled, but not completely convinced.

"I," she said to herself with conviction, "am taking this to New York."

Jane waited anxiously for her parents to return home. As soon as they did, she explained everything to them. They quickly retrieved the picture as Mark stared in astonishment at it. Mrs. McTerm immediately wrapped it up, but they would not hear of Jane going to New York by herself to turn the picture in. Jane pleaded with her parents until an idea struck her. Heather could come with her. Jane couldn't wait to ask her, when she suddenly remembered that Heather was on crutches and therefore couldn't come. Her mind rolled over other ideas until she thought of Diana. Diana had turned eighteen three weeks ago and she would be like an adult. Mrs. McTerm was beginning to soften when she heard that because it was true. Plus, Diana was responsible and it would just be a day trip.

Jane knew she was winning the argument when her parents started to ask her questions like, "Would you be careful?" and, "You wouldn't have to miss school, right?"

"You sure you wouldn't have to stay overnight?" was the last question Jake asked before both parents caved in completely.

"Heather won't be able to come; she's on crutches!" Jane yelled to her mom from another room.

"Just ask Diana then!" her mom yelled back.

Jane dialed Diana's phone number; when Diana answered she seemed tired and bored.

"Diana, are you sick or something?"

"No, I'm fine. I just have nothing to do. Hey, would you like to come over to my house for a little?"

"Sure."

"All right. You can come now."

"Okay, bye."

Jane hung up the phone and looked out the window once more. Ever since she had called Barry, something started to swell inside her like someone had suddenly flicked on a light switch that lit up an otherwise dim room. She knew that what she had could change the entire court case and put the rightful people in jail. But Jane still wasn't sure what significance her picture held on the case or who the "rightful people" should be. Her mind raced in a thousand directions as the raindrops grew heavier, weighing the tree limbs down and pushing the grass into the slushy mud. Jane turned away from the window, ran downstairs, and put a raincoat on.

"Where are you going?" asked Mrs. McTerm.

"I'm going over to Diana's."

"I'm going with you because I have to go to the store after."

Jane gave her mom an odd look.

"We are taking the car, right?" she asked.

"I was planning on walking."

"Walking! Diana's house is too far away."

"Not that far," Jane shrugged.

"It's pouring rain! Come on, I'll let you drive."

Jane was instantly convinced. She grabbed her permit, and they left.

Jane was a fairly good driver; she tired hard to impress her mom whenever she was allowed to drive. She would be able to get her license in two weeks and under the present conditions, Jane was extra cautious of the slippery roads.

"Okay, bye, Jane," Mrs. McTerm said as Jane pulled into Diana's driveway.

"Bye, Mom," Jane replied as her mom climbed into the driver's seat.

After Mrs. McTerm had driven away, Jane rang the doorbell.

"Hi, Jane. Come in," Diana's mom said.

Heather had been up in her room staring at the poem, pondering over what it might mean. Even though her mom had told her that the poem meant nothing and not to worry about it, she sat there at her desk trying to get some sense out of it. She tried to take it apart, look at each sentence by itself, but she still could not understand it.

Heather read it to herself for the umpteenth time:

"Some have been told
As this story will unfold
Made from crooks
Your friends will suffer
But you already know this
From no other."

"Heather, are you still up in your room?"

"Yes, Mom."

"Heather, darling, I've started to worry about you. Come downstairs and stop thinking about that silly poem. I made you a snack."

Not wanting to disappoint her mom, Heather laid the piece of paper on her desk and preceded downstairs.

I tired to fix my faults, but the sun has set and it will never rise again.

Chapter 9

Jane was having a hard time convincing Diana to go with her. Diana just didn't seem to have the same perspective as Jane.

"Look, Diana, why don't you want to come?"

"Jane, what if this isn't the right picture? We could get into serious trouble."

"I don't understand! A free chance to visit New York and hand in a vital piece of evidence to a courthouse that could change the course of the case, doesn't that sound important?"

"Well, I don't know. How would this even change things?"

Jane thought about that for a moment before answering. "Diana, someone must have tampered with the evidence. This could show that Sam Norman really couldn't be placed at my aunt's house that...night."

"Sorry, Jane, I didn't mean to make things hard for you. I just always thought that New York could be confusing, and there's so many people."

"You're wrong, Diana, very wrong. It's easy to get around New York, and we wouldn't even be staying overnight."

"Will we have time to shop?"

"I guess, maybe in a store or two."

Diana looked up at her ceiling and replied in exasperation, "Since

I know you won't stop asking until I say yes, if my mom says it's alright, I guess I'll go."

"Great!" Jane could hardly keep herself from falling off Diana's bed.

"Calm down, we need to think about this."

"I'm just a little relieved."

"Really?" Diana's tone was flat and dripped with sarcasm. "Jane, we need to handle the picture carefully if it's as important as you say it is, but I just want to get this over with. When would we be leaving?"

Jane thought about the question before answering, "Tomorrow, it's a Wednesday, right?"

"Yep."

"Why don't you ask your mom if you can go?"

"Yeah, I'll be back in a minute."

Diana left Jane to wait in her room.

Several posters had been hung up in various parts of Diana's room. A shelf with all her jewelry had been placed above her full-length mirror. Her bed was to the right of the door. Next to Diana's bed was a small wooden nightstand. It had one drawer, which had a combination lock on it. On top of the nightstand were a small lamp and a book. The book looked of medium-length judging by its size, but the bookmark in it was fairly close to the beginning. Jane turned around and looked out Diana's window. Rain was still pouring down onto the ground and churning up mud. It gave her a drowsy feeling.

Jane sighed; she felt quite tired. "Must be the rain," she thought to herself.

Diana reentered her room. "My mom said she's not sure. She wants to talk to your parents first."

"That's better than no. Maybe you and your parents can come and have dinner at my house."

"Ask," Diana said as she handed Jane the phone.

Jane's parents were very much obliged to the idea of having Diana and her parents come. In fact, they seemed more excited than Jane.

At around 7:45, Jane, Diana, and Diana's parents drove over to the McTerms'. Diana's mom took some wrong turns because she was so accustomed to driving to Jane's old house, and that made them about ten minutes late.

Jane still felt mixed emotions about her new house, but she couldn't help loving all the open space she had just to think. Like a dream, she felt suspended over everything, just floating and looking down at what use to be.

After parking, they walked inside and were escorted to the dining room. Diana sat next to Jane and continued to inquire about their trip. "Jane, are we even allowed to take this in ourselves?

"All we're doing is handing it in."

"Is there like, gonna be any danger involved in our trip?"

"Shouldn't be."

"When are we leaving?"

"My dad said there's a bus leaving at 8:30 and 10:30. Which one do you want to take?"

"10:30, definitely. I won't be up till 9:30 at the earliest."

"Okay." Jane sounded a little disappointed.

"What's the rush anyway?"

Before Jane could answer, Mrs. McTerm yelled from the kitchen, "Jane, phone!"

"All right, Mom!" Jane yelled back. She leaned over and reached for the cordless phone Mike was holding. "Hello."

"Hey, Jane. How ya doing?"

Jane immediately knew who it was. "Hi, Leea. I'm fine. How are you?"

Leea used to live right next door to Jane; they were each other's company as young children. When Leea turned five, she moved to Texas as Jane moved to New Jersey. Leea's parents decided to divorce, but she and Jane always managed to keep in touch. Leea's mom, Rachell, had a sister that lived in Texas so they moved down there to live with her. Right when Leea's mom had a full time job and was starting to earn money, her sister received a job transfer and was forced to take it. Now, Leea and her mom live in the small house in Texas by themselves. Without her sister to pay for half the mortgage, they had trouble making ends meet. Leea became employed at a part time job after school. She and her mom had become very close, even though Leea has evolved into an extremely independent person.

"I'm fine, Jane. You haven't written anything for almost two weeks now. What's wrong?"

"Nothing's wrong; I've just been busy."

"Ever since your aunt died you haven't called. Are you sure you're okay?"

"No, Leea, it isn't anything like that. It's..." Jane paused. Her mind wanted to keep everything a secret, but something else tugged inside her. She just felt like it was her responsibility to tell Leea. Leea knew everything that went on in Jane's life, and Jane didn't see any real reason why telling her would result in negative reactions.

"Leea, can you keep a really important secret?"

"Course, 'cause I would never tell nothing I'm not supposed to."

"All right, remember when I told you about my aunt?"

"Yeah," she replied glumly, "I remember."

"Just a little while ago when we were moving into our new home, my brother found this picture. It was of my two cousins. It's the same one being used in the case, but it has a different date. Mine proves the man accused was not really there that night and that the prosecution handed in false evidence."

"What are you going to do with it?"

"Bring it to the courthouse and let them send it to labs."

"What are the prosecutors' names?"

"The side that presented the picture? Umm, their names are Tom Hankar and Joe Tremmer. I think they framed Sam Norman."

"Maybe."

"Probably."

"Okay, Jane, I have to go now. That's really unbelievable; call me later."

"Alright. Bye, Leea."

"Bye."

Diana stared oddly at Jane. "You never told me you had a friend named Leea."

"I guess I didn't think of it."

The dining room was set as lovely as Jane had ever seen it. Porcelain plates lay next to the perfectly folded napkins. On the table was a basket of rolls and ice water. The over-hanging chandelier was sparkling as the fading light from the windows fell lightly on it.

The dinner went impressively well. Jane held her breath the entire time. When Jane's and Diana's parents first began chatting, the conversation was only about what had been happening the past few weeks and how work was going. Jane was beginning to wonder if her mom was going to talk about the trip at all, but eventually it came up. Jane tried to mention "day trip" as much as possible. After awhile, Jane was getting tired of answering the endless amount questions about what she would be doing there and what Barry Lonad had instructed. Mr. McTerm said he would call Barry and confirm everything. It was all worth it in the end because on Wednesday, Jane and Diana would be going to New York.

Each singular action is not placed in a solitary chamber. It takes the hand of the next event and pushes on until it has created the future of its creator.

Chapter 10

The night was dwindling on, and dark clouds had descended over the sky, covering up the full moon. The stars appeared as tiny diamonds suspended over the inky blackness, the eternal blackness, covering up far-off whispers and hidden secrets never to be discovered.

Heather turned her head away from her window. She glanced at her clock; it read 10:23 p.m. Yawning, she hopped over to her bed, balancing on her good ankle. Lying down, she pulled the blankets up to her chin. There was a strong will in her that fought her tried eyes from closing. She didn't want to have another dream even though they seemed so meaningless. They had some sense to them, and Heather had this feeling that she didn't want to find out what it was. As the moon rose higher, sleep overcame her, and with it came the dreams.

Swirling colors, dark and forbidding, came, as noises she had never heard before screamed from all directions. Everything felt so real. Blinding fog surrounded her, and it was hard to think or breathe. Surrounded by colors, she couldn't move. They were blocking her. Then the thing that scared her most came, the one thing that she couldn't lay her eyes on.

"How come you did nothing?" the voice said accusingly.

"What do you mean?" Heather tried to yell back, but there were too many colors, too much fog. She couldn't talk; she couldn't even hear herself think.

"You do not understand the poem. You are not trying. This is now your fault," the voice said flatly, not even raising its tone.

Everything grew silent, and something terrible started to happen. Heather felt a tightening around her neck like a cold hand had gripped her from behind. She was trapped in the colors, and she couldn't free herself. Trying wildly to breathe in, she thrashed her arms all around her. No air was coming in, and she started to see new colors. A panic rose within her. The fog grew thicker and tiny stars exploded in front of her.

"Air. I need air!" She tried to yell but couldn't. The air grew tighter. All she could hear was the voice, laughing with a dry whisper.

With one final effort, she thrust herself sideways and like a miracle, she was thrown back into reality. That's when she realized that she had been laying with her face in her pillow. Her heart was almost pounding out of her chest, and she bent over, trying to fill her lungs with the fresh air.

"Just my pillow," she whispered to herself. "Not real."

She closed her eyes and breathed in a sigh of relief. Opening them, she stumbled out of bed and hobbled over to her desk. She picked up the piece of paper with the mysterious poem on it. After observing it for a moment she leaned over to her garbage can and let go. As it floated to the bottom, Heather stared, mystified. It seemed to be floating in slow motion, and once it hit the bottom, a loud thud was issued from the inside of the can. Startled, Heather leaned in closer to have a better look. Her eyes grew wide with a steady fear that clutched her still-recovering heart. The words on the paper seemed to have vanished. One line was left, but it didn't even look like Heather's handwriting anymore. It was scratchy and thin. It read, "Your friends will suffer." Heather lunged for the paper and grabbed it out of her garbage can. Placing it on her desk, she glanced at her clock, and then back at the paper. The poem was identical to the copy Heather had first written, like nothing had changed.

"Maybe it just fell sideways and I couldn't see the rest of the words." Heather tried to reason with herself. A cold breeze touched her neck, and she whirled around to find her window cracked open. She felt so scared inside that she just wanted everything in her house to stop creaking and the wind to stop blowing. Suddenly, something within her filled with rage. She didn't understand why this was happening. Why she had to be terrified about nothing, about something she didn't even understand, something she didn't even want to understand. Heather snapped; she picked up her porcelain lamp with all her might. Raising it above her head, she smashed it with a strong fearful might, against her wall. The noise was so loud that she even scared herself, and immediately after she had done it, she regretted it. Her mom came bursting into her room screaming, "Heather!"

"I'm fine, Mother," Heather said, shaking.

"Oh my gosh! What happened to your lamp?"

"I'll explain in a moment," Heather replied. "Or at least try to," she whispered under her breath.

"Was there a burglar? Should I call the police?"

"No, Mom. Let's work on getting all this painful glass out of my cast first. I'll explain, don't worry."

Heather tried over and over to explain to her mom why she had thrown a one hundred and fifty dollar lamp at her wall but it was no use; she just couldn't understand.

"Let me get this straight, you smashed your lamp against the wall because of a nightmare?"

"It wasn't the nightmare; it was what was happening to me."

"Which would be?"

"Well, it's kind of hard to explain."

"Every question I have asked you tonight has started with 'it's hard to explain'! If you think that this is to hard for me to understand, maybe a therapist will. I'm calling one tomorrow as soon as it's light out."

"Mom, it's not that complicated!"

"Apparently it is if you're, you're afraid to lay down in case you fall asleep and you're breaking things! Look, I don't want to fight with you, Heather! Just try to get some sleep or whatever and tomorrow we will go and see someone."

"Mom you don't..."

"No arguing!"

Heather sat on her couch waiting for the sun to rise. She sat there for quite some time just thinking about the events of the past few weeks. Most importantly, what these nightmares had to do with anything and why they started after Jane's aunt was murdered. The only clue that Heather could actually touch was the poem.

Jane couldn't sleep, either, but it wasn't from nightmares. She lay in her bed staring at her ceiling and listening to her clock as the minutes slowly passed by. She was so full of excitement she could barely lay still. Jane felt an overwhelming sense of duty, and she knew how important it was that she do everything right. Stepping out of bed, she began packing things into her backpack that Diana and she would need for the next day. As the time rolled on, she settled back into bed, convincing herself that she needed sleep for her trip.

"...I'll be careful." Sometimes it just doesn't matter if you're careful. Your actions are already in order.

Chapter 11

Jane slipped her backpack on her shoulders and ran downstairs; only forty-five more minutes until she would leave.

"Mom, is Diana here yet?"

"Not yet, Jane, she won't be here for another fifteen minutes. Here, eat some breakfast," Mrs. McTerm said as she took a plate from Maribell when she walked by.

"I'm not hungry, Mom. I'm too nervous."

"I know you are, and remember how important what you're doing really is. Please, I want you to be really careful and..."

"I know, Mom, I'll be careful."

Ring! Ring! Ring!

"Hello?" Jane said as she picked up the kitchen phone.

"Hi, Jane, right?"

"Yeah, it's me."

"I was wondering if you could come to my house and pick me up because my brother took my car and my mom's still sleeping and..."

"That's fine, Diana. We'll pick you up."

"Thanks. I'm almost ready; I just have to get dressed."

"Get dressed! You're not even dressed yet?"

"Hey, we don't have to leave for like, another half hour. Plus, don't push it, Jane, you know I'm apprehensive about going. Come pick me up and I'll be ready."

"All right."

"Bye."

Jane sat down at the kitchen table and stared out her kitchen window. Today would be a fine day, not like before. The storm had passed on, leaving a light sun and quiet breeze that made the trees sway softly from side to side. Patches of gray shadows covered Jane's lawn, but the long-awaited sunshine brought tiny birds to glide above her home. As the sun's rays grew stronger, it turned its bright, fiery gaze onto the treetops, making the leafy patterns grow darker.

Jane leaned her head on the kitchen table. She felt fatigued from staying up half the night, and soon her eyes drooped shut and sleep took over her senses.

"Jane! Jane, where are you! It's time to leave!"

"What? Dad, I didn't hear you."

"Jane, it's time to leave; get in the car."

"Coming." Jane slipped her backpack on and was about to go out the front door when she heard the phone ring. Questioning whether or not she should go back and answer it, she heard her dad yell from the car, "Jane, let the answering machine get it! Come on! We're already late!"

Jane jumped into the car and they drove over to Diana's house. After picking her up, they raced down to the bus stop.

"I was thinking, there is no reason why I shouldn't come. It would probably make things a heck of a lot easier. Are you sure you'll be o.k. by yourselves?" asked Jake worriedly.

"Yes, Dad, I'm sure. I'm almost eighteen, and I can take care of myself. We will be fine. Bye."

"Alright, bye."

"Bye, Mr. McTerm!" added Diana as he drove away.

"Do you have a watch?" asked Jane.

"No," replied Diana.

"Great! Neither do I," Jane said harshly.

"Don't get so upset over nothing, Jane. We'll just have to ask people."

"I guess so."

With a few moments to spare, Jane and Diana sat down on an old rusty bench. Half its paint had been worn off and all the metal discolored. One leg was off, but the rest were nailed to the ground to keep it from toppling over. Feeling drowsy from being jerked awake and rushed, Jane sat down wearily, waiting for the bus.

Mr. McTerm arrived back home at the same time the bus came to pick up Jane and Diana. After parking his car in the garage, he went inside. About to go and find out where his two sons were, he remembered that there should be a message on the answering machine.

He walked over to the machine and pressed play. The person talking sounded distraught and upset, "Listen, Jane, if you're there...I hope you are. Anyway, I don't think you should go to the courthouse. I've had this uncanny feeling, and I think we should leave this matter with the police. I'm really serious. Jane, please don't go. Ah, I don't know if.... you're still here. Call me....please, it's Heather."

Mr. McTerm stared at the answering machine for a moment, undecided about what he should do. Picking up a phone book, he located Heather's phone number and dialed.

He hung up with a sigh. No answer.

Heather and her mom had not talked much that morning. Her mother seemed too confused, and Heather just didn't know what to say. Her mom drove down the highway on the long trip to the psychiatrist when Heather finally spoke up, her voice small and half mumbled, "Mom, I don't want to go to that place."

"Heather, I said no arguing."

"What will I say?"

"Whatever you have on your mind."

"Why can't I just tell you?"

"That doesn't seem to work real well, dear." Mrs. Learl's voice was tight and she spoke with failing conviction.

"What do you mean?"

"After you showed me that poem, you had been acting, well,

different. I tried to talk to you, tell you it was nothing, and the next thing I know my extremely expensive lamp is broken."

"Oh yeah, sorry about that."

"Sorry indeed," her mom said softly as they pulled into the parking lot.

The psychiatrist's office smelled of must and Pine Sol. It had a mix of comfort and desolation. There was a huge window that covered about three-quarters of one of the walls. It had no blinds, but it owned huge, dark velvet curtains that overlapped as they touched the floor. The carpet was the same color, a deep cherry red. The lamps hung from the ceiling, therefore preventing the whole room from being lit. Patches of darkness slipped into the corners and had woven themselves into the sides of paintings and chairs that were scattered across the room.

Heather and her mom stood awkwardly in the center of the room. They didn't know if they should sit, stand or converse. Eventually, a lady entered. She was dressed sharply in a savvy pinstripe skirt suit and looked extremely comforting and smart. The only thing that identified her as an employee was a tag she wore on her shirt that read, "Julie Spearogotis, psychiatrist." Her dirty-blonde hair was pulled up in a messy bun, and her dark brown eyes never stopped moving. When she spoke, her voice sounded intelligent but inviting. "This should be Heather, correct?"

Heather just nodded.

"Alright, first of all I'd like to talk to Heather alone. So, if Mom could please step outside and wait in the lobby, we can get started."

Heather's mom obliged.

"Heather, why don't you have a seat over there?" She pointed to an over-stuffed shiny chair that was in the middle of the room. The psychiatrist pulled a chair over from the opposite side of the room and put it next to Heather's for herself.

"Heather, can you explain why you are here? Not just that someone made you come, but why he or she did. Please, be honest."

Heather took a deep breath and spoke, "This is why I am here." She paused and thought, how can I tell her without bringing up Jane and the picture? Will Jane get mad if I tell? Heather began speaking again. "Do you keep everything secret?"

"Always."

"Good. This all started when my friend's aunt died."

Chapter 12

Jane and Diana strolled up to the courthouse where the trial was being held. They were about to walk in when a guard appeared, seemingly out of nowhere.

"And where are you two ladies going?"

"We need to turn in a piece of evidence to the court."

"What? What are you girls taking about? I haven't heard about this. Plus, all evidence is turned into the labs first, not the courtroom," the man voiced sternly.

"We know," Jane said slowly, "but Barry Lonad said that we were supposed to come here."

"I don't suppose you're talking about the Myrtle McTerm case."

"Yes, we are and she is...was my aunt."

"Is that so?" The guard eyed Jane and with a slightly softer tone added, "Well, hold on. I'll check and see if someone knows anything about you two, and if they don't, I can't let you in without proper ID."

"Fine." Jane turned as the guard entered the courthouse.

Diana looked questionably over Jane's shoulder and spoke softly as if trying to keep something a secret. "Jane, there're two guys standing behind a tree over there. I think they've been listening to us. Here they come."

Jane whirled around. Sure enough there were two men trying to hide behind a nearby oak tree. The shorter one kept falling out of the slim hiding place and was finally pushed forcefully forward as his taller accomplice saw the girls staring at them. Attempting to maintain their dignity, the two men brushed themselves off nonchalantly and proceeded toward the girls. One was tall and built sturdily with light brown hair, and the other was shorter and looked less menacing but had mischievous hazel eyes that watched Jane closely.

"I know those guys."

"From where, Jane?"

Before Jane could answer, the two men were standing directly in front of them, less than two feet away.

The shorter of the two spoke. "We just happened to overhear you two talking to Chris Eian. He's a nice guy. What is it you want to show him?"

Diana panicked as she suddenly recognized the two men. She stood rooted to the spot. She was far more afraid than Jane, and it showed.

Jane held the box that contained the framed picture tightly to her. Diana leaned over and whispered in Jane's ear, "Jane, give it to them, they could be dangerous. I'm scared."

The taller man leaned over and snatched the box from Jane as she listened to Diana. Before Jane could retaliate, the man had opened it and stared hard at the picture. He squinted while holding it close, then he held it out and just kept staring at it. Jane couldn't quite make out the conversation, but she listened intently.

Motioning to his partner, he said in disbelief, "Hey, Joe have a look at this. I thought that you'd....what kind of an ignorant, oafish, unreliable son of....are you! Man, if we don't destroy this...." Right as the taller guy leaned over to show him the picture, Jane grabbed Diana's hand, snatched the picture from the taller man, whose fingers slipped on the glass frame, and ran.

"Where are we going, Jane?"

"I don't know, Diana, but we can't stay here!"

Jane felt an icy tug at her heart. She didn't know these men, all she knew was that they could be guilty, guilty of murder. Their feet pounded the ground. You could hear their breath, hoarse and ragged. Neither of them were very good runners, and soon the two men caught up with them. They roughly grabbed Jane's arm, and she lost balance and hit the pavement, bruising the right side of her face. Diana pulled and kicked to get out of their grasp, but there was no competition; they wouldn't let go. Before either of them had the chance to scream, they were pushed gruffly into a dark blue car that sped off in a hurry. But there was one more witness to the scene—the guard had come out of the courthouse.

Running immediately after the car, Chris turned onto a street that led to only two possible places, a park or a small landing site that only lunched private jets and small planes.

The blue car pulled to a stop and all four occupants either stepped out or were jerked out. Tom had Jane's arms pulled behind her back, and Joe had a tight grip on Diana. Jane stared up at a plane that looked like a petite jet. Before she could think anymore on the subject, the taller man spoke.

"If you give that picture back to me, we'll forget this whole thing happened."

"Who are you? I don't understand. Why is this picture so important to you two men?" Jane said in a puzzled tone.

Diana looked at Jane, bewildered.

Jane shot Diana a slim smile, then stared at the two men as if waiting for an answer.

"Of course you know who we are."

"No, I, ah, I don't think so."

The two men stared at each other.

"I'm Joe and this is Tom," Joe said impatiently.

"No, I still don't recognize you. Am I supposed to know who you are?"

"I don't know where you're going with this, but we just want that picture," Joe said.

"This is for those people in the courthouse. You might know them. Their names are Tom Hankar and Joe Tremmer."

"That's us!" Tom said angrily as he twisted Jane's arms harder.

"How do I know it's you? You could be trying to trick me. This is a very important piece to the court case, and if I were to give it to the wrong people...well, it would be devastating." Jane fought to control her pain.

Diana thought, "Buying time, Jane?" She added, "But for what?"

"I refuse to give it to anyone besides Tom Hankar and Joe Tremmer," Jane persisted.

Joe whispered to Tom, "Whoever they are, they're not trying to get us in trouble, because they were going to give it to us anyway." He turned to Jane and said, "I'm telling you for the last time to give us that picture!"

Jane's adrenaline was going through the roof, but she hid it well. "No," she replied sharply.

Tom and Joe were fuming inside, but before they could add to the conversation, Chris Eian had caught up with them.

"Hello, Chris. What can I do for you today?" Tom said as he let go of Jane so fast that she fell onto one knee, surprised.

"I would like to know why those girls aren't waiting for me outside the courthouse," Chris answered, panting.

"Well...," the shorter man started to say while loosening his grip on Diana.

"They took us!" Diana yelled out.

"Excuse me?" Chris said in a confused tone.

"They did. They want our evidence. They're criminals!" Diana choked out.

"What are you talking about?" Tom said as he turned his head to glare at Diana.

"Look, I don't know what's going on, but I need the piece of evidence that the girls wanted to hand in," Chris said demandingly.

Joe had lowered the stairs on the jet and was proceeding to pull the girls none-too-nicely toward it.

"We would be happy to carry on this conversation some other time, but we are flying these girls back to their home."

"You know how to fly a plane?" Jane said, craning her neck

sideways to face Joe.

"Tom does."

"You can not leave! Plus, you guys never fly that thing. What happened to the piece of evidence? Chris said, now highly perplexed.

Just as they were being pulled up into the jet, the photograph fell out of Jane's jacket.

Chris walked up to the object and picked it up. He stared at it for a moment and then took out his walkie-talkie. "Hello? This is Chris. Is anyone there?"

There was a moment's pause before a reply came back, "Yes, someone's here. Hey, Chris, have you seen Tom Hankar and Joe Tremmer today? I can't find them. They should have been here a while ago."

Chris lowered his tone to a flat whisper, "Yes, I have. In fact, that's why I called. Something unusual has been going on. Tom and Joe took these two girls up to their private jet and have been trying to avoid conversation with me. I think I know what's happening. Tom and Joe have taken the picture."

"What picture?" the voice said through the walkie-talkie.

"Uh, the key piece of evidence to..."

"That picture? Why would they take that?! They were the ones who handed it in!"

"The other thing is these two girls were holding the picture. I think the girls were trying to steal it, but that's just a guess. I have no idea what's going on, but could you send some back-up? I don't know what to expect. I'm at the landing site just five minutes from here."

"Sure, I'll have a police car come down. I'm sure there's nothing to worry about."

"Yeah, thanks," Chris said slowly as he turned off his walkie-talkie.

Joe thought he had heard everything, but he had only heard the part about sending more policemen, and thinking that Chris was on to them, he felt a panic inside. As Chris went to turn around, Joe hit him with the nearest thing to him, a metal trash can. Following the crash of the hollow trash can, Chris fell to the floor with a thud.

"Tom, we have to get out of here. The police are coming; you know the girls will tell! What should we do?"

"I wish I knew how the hell they gained so much information! We can't just get rid of them now! We'll have to do it later!"

Jane and Diana's eyes widened. They clung to each other in the back of the plane, terrified.

"Bring Chris up on the plane. We can't leave him here; we don't want things to get any worse. Come on, we're getting out of here!" Tom replied in a bewildered and infuriated voice.

The foreshadowing has come to a halt and now the world has caught up with it.

Chapter 13

"Heather, dear, your story is quite remarkable. Are you sure you're not stretching the truth just a little?"

Heather stared up at the psychiatrist. She had hoped that she would understand. Even though it did not surprise her that she didn't. She had just hoped so much. She had wanted her to understand in the worst way.

Heather stared at her name tag; it swayed back and forth on her blazer. Julie Spearogotis, Julie Spearogotis, Julie Spearogotis, read over and over in Heather's mind.

"Heather?"

"Ms. Spearogotis, could you recommend a psychiatrist that will believe my story?"

"Heather, I believe you, but you have to understand how many people come in here and tell me the tallest tales. They tell the most ridiculous stuff. I believe that you are under stress and possibly hallucinating. For us to work on this problem, you need to understand what is really wrong with you and prove to me that you know your situation."

"How can I prove that I had a dream and started suffocating? How can I prove that when I went horseback riding through the woods I got this unearthly feeling inside me?"

"Heather, this is something that is very typical when it comes to paranoia. I don't think you're understanding what I'm saying."

"Wait, look at this." Heather pulled out the poem, the poem that she had heard in some evil nightmare. She knew it didn't prove anything, but maybe Ms. Spearogotis could make some sense out of it. Heather handed the piece of paper over.

Ms. Spearogotis read it thoroughly and then said, "What does this mean?"

"I don't know. I heard it in a dream of mine. I can't make anything out of it. But it won't let me forget about it. There's something about that poem, something that keeps me up at night, something that won't let me be me, something that sticks in the back of my mind." Heather then froze. Some small illusion inside her seemed to have crept up and now she just sat there, her lips moving softly, "I can't run faster Jane. I can't, I'm too winded. I'm..." Heather stopped and stared up at the psychiatrist. "What was I just saying? I completely lost my train of thought."

"Maybe we should call it a day. You can go back outside with your mom."

"Okay, bye then."

As they left the room, Heather's mom rose to her feet. "So, how'd it go?"

"Just as I thought," Heather replied.

Before Heather's mom could question her on what she meant by that, Ms. Spearogotis began to speak. "May I have a word with you for a moment please?"

"That means you, mom," Heather whispered.

"Oh, coming," Heather's mom said hastily.

Once they had entered the office, Ms. Spearogotis closed the door and they both sat down.

"I'm sure that you are confused about all this."

"Yes, I am, in fact; Heather never ever acts like this."

"Please explain?"

"She never tells stories and things that aren't true. She would only bother me with things that really would be affecting her."

"I must say that does surprise me. That changes things."

"How so, Ms. Spearogotis?" Mrs. Learl said, trying to mask her ever-increasing nervousness.

"Please, call me Julie."

"Sure."

"Anyway, I had pictured your daughter as a girl that is always trying new things for attention and makes things up just for entertainment. Could be from not having a father around or many other things. In addition, she is showing signs of paranoia, schizophrenia and anxiety. These are only appearing to be mild now."

"No, no. That's not my daughter at all. She's never acted like this before."

"Well, then. Now that I know that, why don't you have at look at this?"

Ms. Spearogotis took the poem out of her pocket and began to read it aloud,

"Some have been told
As this story will unfold
Made from crooks
Your friends will suffer
But you already know this
From no other."

"I've heard that before! Heather won't stop reading it! She thinks it has some hidden meaning to it."

"Do you mind if I hold on to it?"

"No, of course not. Besides, I'm sure Heather has it memorized."

"Thank you, that's all for now."

"Bye, it was nice meeting you."

As they rode home, Heather stared out the car window. Dark clouds had covered the sky once again, and dusk was upon them. Small droplets of water began to cascade onto the car. They zigzagged down the windows, each taking its own route. Heather enjoyed observing the raindrops fall. She liked watching them take new twists and turns at every moment. They would skid across the car window or plunge slowly to the bottom. They never stayed the same shape;

they were constantly changing. Just as Heather was about to close her eyes, her mom began speaking.

"Heather, I know that you felt uneasy about Jane's trip, so when we get home you can call her. She should be back by now."

"Oh, right. Okay, mom."

The telephone rang in the McTerms' home. Mr. McTerm answered it.

"Hello?"

"Hi, this is Heather. Is Jane there?"

"No, she isn't, can I take a message?"

Heather paused. "Shouldn't Jane be back by now?"

"Well, yes, but they probably just wanted to take their time getting back here. I'll have her call you when she gets home."

"Okay, bye."

"Bye."

"Where have Jane and Diana got to?" Mr. McTerm asked worriedly as he hung up the phone.

"How am I supposed to know? It's only 6:30. Let's wait a little longer before we get worried," Mrs. McTerm replied.

"Yeah, I guess so. They're probably just fine and on their way home now," Mr. McTerm sighed.

Underestimating the possible turn of events is easy to do, considering that anything is possible and that that isn't always a good thing.

Chapter 14

Jane opened her eyes; she had finally awoke from her fitful sleep. Taking stock of her surroundings, the first thing she noticed was that she and Diana had been tied to the passenger chairs. The plane was also very small and there was only enough room for six other passengers. She observed Diana, who was still asleep. Jane had lost all track of time. She strained her neck sideways to stare out the window. "Must be night," she thought. The only thing she could see when looking out the window was black. A cold, pitch black etched the outside, making Jane shiver. She couldn't move her hands or feet. They had been tied so tightly that the blood circulation had been cut off. The realization of what was really happening was finally starting to appear in Jane's mind. Murderers had kidnapped them. Jane shivered. She had to talk to someone or she felt she would burst inside. Leaning as far over as she could, she began to nudge Diana.

"What's happening?" Diana yawned.

"Sshhhh. Look Diana, I have no idea where we are, but I do know that we have no way of getting out of here."

"I'm scared, Jane, and I know you are too. I just...."

Before Diana could finish her sentence, Joe came out of the cockpit and into the passenger area.

"Tom says we need more fuel for the plane. Now, we have more barrels of it in the back, so we have to land the plane first before we can add it." Joe stood awkwardly for a moment. "If you feel like we're going to crash, we're not, we're just landing the plane."

Jane looked at Joe with all the humor her heart would let out, for Diana's sake. "Thanks for, ah, clearing that up."

Joe looked at her for a second as if undecided on what to do. Finally he spoke, his voice trying to sound controlling, yet coming off as rather pathetic, "No talking! If I hear one more word, you'll, you'll....be sorry!"

"How much more sorry could I be?"

"You, stop asking questions!" With that, Joe left the room.

"I don't think either of them know what they're doing," Jane whispered.

Diana's smile turned serious as she whispered back to Jane, "I know, but that can be bad too. That one, Joe, he seems like a follower and isn't that bright or witty or dangerous. It's the other one that I'm afraid of. Don't talk to him like that, no matter what."

"Don't worry, I've been paying attention to their actions. I know Tom's dangerous and he seems to be at his wits end too. I'm worried, though, not so much of this moment, but how things will end." Jane let her voice trail off. She just couldn't tell Diana how she really felt. She had to only show her brave emotions, and it was tearing her apart inside.

"Hey, these are just double knots pulled tight," Diana observed as she stared down at her bindings.

"Why did you just tell me that?" Jane asked.

"Oh, ah, well, no special reason, just trying to make conversation." Diana stared at Jane, waiting for her to pick up what she just said, but Jane didn't even show any interest.

Jane sighed and looked out the window as she saw the ground draw nearer.

It was still pitch black when the plane landed safely to the ground. Tom and Joe passed by the girls but paid no heed to them. They returned rather quickly, each pulling a barrel toward the main exit. Jane strained her ears to try and hear the conversation that was passing between the two men.

"Tom, you turned the plane off, right?"

"Right."

"Have the keys?"

"No, I left them on the seat but that doesn't matter."

"How much fuel do you want to put in?"

"At least a barrel and a half."

"Do you know what we should do with these girls?"

"Actually Joe, I've got a pretty good plan."

"Yeah, what?"

"We leave them here in the middle of this God-forsaken desert or take one of Chris's guns, finish 'em, leave 'em and then go back to New York. We'll make up some excuse for our absence and..."

"Everything's back on track," Joe said, cutting him off.

Jane looked at Diana. "This doesn't sound so bad; they're going to let us go."

"What are you taking about, Jane? We don't know where we are; we're defiantly not anywhere near civilization. At least there is water on this plane, even though we can't get at it, and plus, it looks like they're leaning toward the second suggestion."

"I'm almost all untied," Jane whispered.

"I thought you weren't even listening to me before."

"That's because I heard them coming. I just can't untie my own wrists. Diana, can you reach my bonds?"

"What?"

"The rope that I'm tied to," Jane rephrased.

"Well, I think so."

"Good, untie them."

"But, but, why? I mean..."

"Just do it!" Jane said harshly.

Diana swallowed hard and obliged.

It was extremely difficult at first because Diana couldn't see what see was doing, and she could barely feel anything since her hands were tied up, too. As Diana worked away at the rope, the numbness in her hands grew into sharp needles striking her. After a bit of tugging, it slowly became looser, and finally Jane's hands were free.

Jane winced as the blood began to circulate again; it was quite painful. As soon as the throbbing began to disappear, Jane tugged furiously at the rope that held her ankles to the chair.

"Yes!" Jane said almost too loud as the rope finally gave way. Wiping sweat from her forehead, she stood up, then fell down.

"Are you okay?" Diana said, still tied down.

"Yes, it's just my feet. I've got to wait for the blood to start flowing first."

"Jane, you're untied; now what are you going to do?"

"I was listening to them talking; they left the keys on the pilot seat."

"Jane we don't know anything about planes." But Diana's voice was lost on Jane as she began to half-stumble, half-crawl toward the cockpit.

Jane was now sitting on the pilot's seat. She held the key in her hand. It was hard for her to keep from trembling. Trying to see the pedals under the steering wheel in the dim light was very difficult. She finally placed her foot lightly on the one she hoped was the acceleration. Jane felt a deep freeze like pounding in her stomach; swallowing hard, she put the key in the keyhole and waited for the right moment. She could hear Tom and Joe's voice faintly from outside.

"No wonder you were carrying that barrel so easily. It's got nothing in it!"

"You shouldn't be talkin', Tom, yours was barely full!"

"Well, at least mine had something in it! Do you remember if there were any more back there?"

"Yeah, I think so."

"Good, go get it!"

"Why don't you?"

"Because I already bought out fuel, you just brought out a barrel!"

"Fine, fine, fine," Joe grumbled, then added, "Don't shout so loud, don't want anyone to hear us."

"Idiot! Who's gonna hear us! There's no one for miles around, and hurry up with that barrel!"

It was now or never for Jane. She tried to turn the key, but it was harder than she had thought. Her fingers, covered in perspiration, slipped across the key. Turning her head to look at the floor and take a deep breath, she tired to refocus. Suddenly, her eyes came in contact with a corner of the picture that was sticking out of a suit jacket which lay in a heap on the floor. With a new courage, she turned the key sideways and a massive roar issued from the engine. For a second it scared Jane and she fought to keep the terror locked inside her. Jane pushed down on the pedal. She saw the plane moving slowly forward. The numbness in her hands made her fingers slip hard, and the steering wheel turned slightly. Puzzled on why she couldn't turn the wheel completely, she banished the thought from her mind. After a few seconds, the plane increased its speed, and she put all her weight on the pedal. The plane shot forward. Taking the steering wheel, she began to push it down as she saw the plane tilt up. She could hear loud shouts from outside as the plane lifted off the ground. Jane's heart was pounding and her face covered in sweat, almost blinding her vision despite the cool air that came rushing out of the still-open cockpit door.

Jane's hands were still paralyzed, but she did the best she could to hold the steering wheel steady.

Turning her head, Jane yelled toward the direction of Diana, "Diana, Diana! I did it. I'm flying!"

"Oh my God, Jane! Do you think you could turn it around? We can backtrack to New York or someplace close and find help on landing this thing!" You could detect the excitement in Diana's voice, the feeling that it was almost over.

Jane stared at the steering wheel as the cold realization of what Tom had said hit her. "No, I left them on the seat but that *doesn't* matter." Then Jane's voice answered back more afraid than excited, "What are those things called that people put on cars so if someone tries to steal it they can't move the steering wheel? You know, it looks like a steal rod!" The scream of the engine muffled Jane's shaking voice.

"I don't what they're called!" Diana yelled back.

"Do you know how to get one off?"

"No!" Diana replied slowly.

Jane's voice was shrill. "They put one on the steering wheel and I can't turn the plane!"

Luck and chance have different motives. Luck ties in with complete bewilderment that grabs you suddenly, while chance is a risk that you are already aware of. The same predicament has people looking at different views. Some occurrences are found out by luck and some by chance.

Chapter 15

Early morning had arrived, bringing with it late-night mist and a soft, unsure sun. Deep clouds suppressed the dawning light, tearing it down with shady, black shadows, shadows that surfaced on the McTerm's lawn and saddened the otherwise brisk day.

Anxiety was harshly eating away at Mrs. McTerm. She and her husband notified Barry Lonad when the girls had not returned as planned, but he was just as puzzled as they were. Mrs. McTerm knew Jane and Diana could have sojourned, but then they would have called. In an attempt to get her mind off the present situation, Mrs. McTerm decided to converse with Maribell, whose occupation was serving as the McTerms' maid. Maribell declined Mrs. McTerm's invitation to have tea at first, claiming she had an exceedingly large number of tasks to attend to. Despite Maribell's statements, Mrs. McTerm convinced her, and within a few minutes they were seated on a cream-colored sofa sipping mint tea.

"How was life in Brazil?"

Maribell swallowed before answering, "I had family there and enjoyed living near them, but I love it in America." A pleasant air floated around her dark, dapper hair that blended in with her delicate eyes and warm smile.

"How long have you been living here?" Mrs. McTerm chatted politely.

"Oh, about four years. I lived in Nebraska for a year before I moved to New Jersey." Mrs. McTerm glanced up from staring at her tea as she detected Maribell's audible accent. Maribell drank the last sip of her tea and rose from her position.

"I must get back to work making the beds. Thank you, the tea was wonderful."

Mrs. McTerm was visibly disappointed; she had been enjoying the conversation immensely.

Perking up a little, Mrs. McTerm walked over toward Maribell. "Maribell, I'm going to help you. You'll have someone to talk to, and besides, I used to do housework all the time. I don't think I'm quite used to having all the cleaning done for me."

Maribell smiled warmly and replied, "If you wish."

Spending most of the day tiding up the rooms, by dinnertime they had the whole house looking spotless.

Mrs. McTerm came bounding cheerfully down the stairs when Jake sullenly pulled her aside. "I'm really getting worried," he sighed wearily.

"Why, dear?" Mrs. McTerm looked puzzled.

"Jane isn't back yet."

Mrs. McTerm's heart sank. She hadn't been thinking about Jane. "She hasn't called or anything, not all day?"

"No, she didn't, I don't know where Jane is."

"Mom, look, there's something on the news about the trial!" Mike and Mark yelled over each other from the kitchen.

She ran into the kitchen with Jake and watched the television intently.

"We have just received word that Tom Hankar and Joe Tremmer are missing. They are the lawyers presently working on the case of Myrtle McTerm. Even more startling, we can't find Chris Eian, the security guard that was on duty around the time they disappeared. All we know now is that Chris Eian called for back-up when he found Joe and Tom at their private jet. Two girls, according to Chris, accompanied them. They have not been identified yet but are missing, too. When we come back, an update on the efforts to stop destruction of the Amazon rainforest."

Mike switched the television off and stood still waiting for his mom to say something. As they stood in silence, the phone rang, and Jake went to pick it up. "Hello Barry," he said into the receiver.

Mystified, Mrs. McTerm finally spoke in a saddened and saturnine voice, "Where are those two girls?"

Jane and Diana were as puzzled as anyone. After Jane had untied Diana, they pondered over their problem; they were flying in one direction. Tom and Joe had securely made sure that while they left the plane to fill the gas tank, no one could turn the steering wheel. Jane had managed to take off without them, but now she was faced with a much larger problem. A problem that swallowed her whole and held her pressed against the wall with nowhere to run; no matter what they did, they couldn't turn the plane. The windows were filled with a pitch black mass that kept the ground far below impossible to view. Nighttime had fallen, and even if they could move the steering wheel to land the plane, they still wouldn't be able to without crashing. Jane's eyes were filled with an uncertain fear. She had put a heavy bag of something on the gas pedal and went to sit by Diana. There was no use trying to pilot the plane; they couldn't do anything. After sitting and doing nothing for about an hour, they both dozed off.

Diana yawned and lazily opened her eyes. The sun was high above them, and a clear blue sky was visible as Diana stared out the cockpit window. As Jane began to wake up, she looked over at Diana, who didn't even glance back at her.

"Hey, Diana, look, there's hardly any clouds." Jane's weak try at making their situation sound casual made things feel even worse. "I feel a little unsure of things. I didn't mean to fall asleep like that. How long do you think we've been sleeping, nine, maybe even ten hours?"

Diana didn't answer. She was still staring out the cockpit window but looking down rather than out at the sky. Diana looked up and said quietly, "Jane, where are we?" As she spoke she motioned for Jane to look outside.

"Oh....my....where...." Jane moved closer to the window and stared down as if trying to get a better view. Her breath was caught inside her and no words could force themselves out. All that was discernible was green. Green. Mist rose in translucent puffs and tropical colored birds soared high above the greenery. Huge vines could be distinguished as they lay above the gigantic masses of trees. The rising sun threw light over patches over the massive forest.

"I, I, I don't know what it is," Jane choked out. She had never witnessed anything more beautiful in her entire life.

"I think it's the Amazon," Diana stated.

"How could it be the Amazon! We would have to be, we would have to be in South America to..."

"We've been flying all night, maybe even longer 'cause of the time change."

"Don't even give me that, Diana! That's crazy! I can't see one house or building from here!"

"Jane, like this past day hasn't been crazy? What else could it be? I've never seen a place like this in New York! It has to be a jungle."

"Well, then, what do we do!?"

"I don't know," Diana said softly, almost hypnotized by the scene below.

Suddenly, they heard a thump that made them shiver. A voice could be heard, and they strained their ears to try to make out the muffled sounds. After hearing the noise, Jane and Diana walked toward the back of the plane where it seemed to be issued. They heard the noise once more; it seemed to be coming from behind a door at the very end of the plane.

Jane knocked on the door and said nervously, "Who's there?"

"Cerrrr," is all Jane and Diana could make out. After thinking for a few moments, Jane looked over at Diana and whispered, "Do you think it's Chris?"

Diana hadn't even thought of that. She had forgotten all about Chris after Joe knocked him unconscious and brought him on the plane. Diana looked back at Jane and nodded her head. Jane carefully opened the closet door and Chris fell down onto the ground, bound and gagged.

Jane and Diana quickly untied him. His hands and feet were numb from the rope cutting off the blood circulation. He moaned as the blood painfully began to course and flow through his choked veins.

Jane untied the gag, and Chris spoke slowly and painfully because his mouth had been badly bruised. "What in the world has happened? The last thing I remember is being hit from behind. I woke up from unconsciousness and everything was black. I guess that was because I was locked in a closet."

"We have a problem," Jane said; she didn't even think of getting reacquainted with him. An icy swelling of fear that had started to grow inside her was turning into a fiery panic. She thought that Chris might have some answers.

"A big, huge problem," added Diana, almost to herself.

Thus Jane began explaining their situation. After she was finished, Chris looked at her and tried to stand up. Leaning on a passenger seat for balance, he gave his thoughts on their predicament. "I can't quite believe all this. But first, if Tom and Joe aren't on the plane anymore, that means that this plane is flying and there's no one in the cockpit?"

"Yeah," Diana answered.

Chris stood there for a moment staring at the two girls, then ran as fast as his aching limbs would allow him into the cockpit. Immediately, he looked out the window, and as Jane and Diana had seen before, there was nothing but a huge tropical jungle. He sat down at one of the chairs and began examining all the dials.

"I don't know much about planes, but I do know how to check fuel and call for help."

Chris began to overlook the seemingly endless amount of switches and dials. He finally put his hand on what looked like a small walkie-talkie. Motioning for Jane and Diana to be silent, he began to push its buttons.

"Hello, is someone there?"

No answer.

"Hello, does anyone copy?"

There was an audible stream of steady static.

Turning some dials and pressing a few more buttons, Chris tried one more time, "Hello, is anyone there?"

A strong male voice broke through the static, "Yes, who is this?"

"This is Chris Eian and I'm flying over some huge, something, a jungle maybe. I don't know how to explain it; I also don't know where I am."

"Is this the Chris Eian that's been missing?"

"Yes, and I need immediate assistance."

"Sorry, didn't copy."

"I need immediate assistance. I'm here with two girls; I don't know where Joe Tremmer and Tom Hankar are, if they're still missing."

"I....hear.....getting.....static....where are..."

"I don't know what the coordinates are! I'm flying over what could be the Amazon rainforest, if we've been flying..." Chris stopped. There was no point. He raised his voice, but it was useless; the radio was too fuzzy to hear anything. Chris checked the fuel and looked up at Jane sharply. "We have a bigger problem than you realize."

"What's wrong?" Jane asked nervously.

"We are reaching zero fuel."

"If we had no fuel, the plane would be crashing." Diana half-laughed, then turned a pale white as the realization of her words hit her.

"Yes. Well, what I meant was it's on zero. We have less than an hour to land this thing."

"How can we land? All there is for miles is green!"

"And don't forget that we can't move the steering wheel!"

Chris stared out the window almost looking for an idea. His face had a tinge of horror, frustration; and the more he looked from the window to Jane and Diana, the more apparent it became.

"Say something, please!" Jane yelled. She needed him to know what to do. He had to know, because she didn't.

"Does this plane have any parachutes on it?"

"What! I'm not jumping out of this plane or any plane, ever!" Diana stated, startled at the implied thought.

"Just in case, we should know, because right now we are in an immense amount of danger."

They started rummaging through the closet until Jane discovered a heavy bag with two parachutes.

"Here, each of you put one on," Chris said as Jane distributed them.

"What about you, you need one." Diana's voice grew faint as her own words echoed around the small room and everyone grew silent. Jane looked from Chris to Diana to the cockpit. Her face lightened as she ran past them into the cockpit. Asking Diana to put her foot on the gas pedal, Jane pulled the heavy bag off of it. Rummaging through it, she pulled out two more parachutes. Once each of them had one on, they went back to the cockpit window and began searching for a place to land. Jane's eyes began to hurt as she stared hard at the green mass. There weren't any brakes in the pattern of green, not even one speck.

Abruptly, a terrible shudder blasted their eardrums as the engine began to sputter and choke. The plane began shaking up and down violently, tossing Jane to the floor.

"We have to jump!" Chris yelled over the loud noise.

"I can't!" Diana yelled back, but Chris already was standing in front of the cockpit door. He had showed them how to use a parachute while they had put them on. He grabbed Jane in one hand and Diana in the other, and it felt like the suspense could rip their pounding hearts apart. Diana's screams of terror could be made out above the roaring noise of the engine, and suddenly all grew quiet. Chris spoke quickly and soft, his heart still pounding feverishly against his chest, "We have to jump, now."

The plane began to tilt downward.

"On three," he yelled.

Jane couldn't hear anything, or at least she had tuned everything out. Looking at Chris, she watched his lips move, *one*, all she could hear or feel was the thud of her heart, and the thrashing of her head pounding against her, *two*, she wanted to scream, "No, don't!" She wanted to....wake up. This can't be happening, this can't be, *three!* Chris closed his eyes and jumped, pulling them out the plane door with him. He clutched their hands tightly. Their shrill screams could be heard above the roaring plane as they plummeted downward.

Jane watched in utter shock as Chris and Diana were torn away from her. She saw Chris go to open his parachute; slightly panicking, she grabbed blindly for her own parachute to open. Taking in a deep breath, she pulled the ripcord with all her might and the parachute flew open. She was jerked upwards but then began to slowly decline. Her pulse had never throbbed or beat that hard, ever. She felt like she was going to burst inside. The pounding inside her head was more than she could bear. Trying to think ahead and rationalize with what was happening only made things worse.

"It's okay, Jane," she said, trying to calm herself, but that was rather impossible for her, and the terror that loomed in her eyes refused to go away. Jane had completely forgotten about the others when she pulled open her parachute, but breathed a hard sigh of relief as she saw two other parachutes not far from her. Jane jerked her head sideways just in time to see the plane as it hit the ground with an enormous crash. A cluster of smoke was hurled into the air as it became apparent that the plane had hit a small lake dead on. A lake that wasn't even visible when Jane was on the plane. Flames rose but quickly retreated as the lake water splashed over it in a colossal wave. Great puffs of black smoke rose and filled the air. Jane, Chris, and Diana were far enough away to avoid the blinding smoke.

"Look how exquisite it is!" Jane exclaimed as they grew closer.

"What? The trees or the beautiful array of carnivores?" Chris yelled so Jane could make out what he was saying.

"Stop, you're scaring me!" Jane yelled back as she took second glances at the scene below.

Jane and Chris were positioned near each other, but Diana was unable to hear their conversation. Jane strained her eyes trying to make out Diana; she seemed so far away. Jane's eyes reluctantly fell onto the impending mass of green as a trance enveloped her senses.

Rich crimson buds took their place among the jungle of surreal vines and lush, colossal trees. From above, the undergrowth could not even be detected as the branches spread their wings, covering what lay beneath. Immense layers of mist filled the air, rising beyond the trees and circling in vitreous puffs. A plentiful amount of brightly colored birds soared above the trees, swooping in and out of view. Of course, it was what was beneath all this that mattered. A place like this could never be justified; each aspect of it was astounding. Its very atmosphere was different from the outside world.

Jane snapped back into awareness when she finally collided into the tops of the trees. The immense trees hung huge vines, big and thick, from nearly every branch. The air was thick and musty. Insects flew everywhere, adding a constant buzzing that wouldn't pause for a heartbeat. The thick, green undergrowth lay beneath them.

Diana struggled to settle herself on the treetops while Jane yelled to Chris, "Chris, we are only about ten yards away from each other, but look at Diana."

"What?" Chris yelled back at Jane. Jane repeated her observation once more, and Chris nodded and turned in Diana's direction.

Diana was positioned about fifty yards away. If they even attempted to get down, they would definitely lose sight of her.

"We have to get down and walk in her direction." Chris yelled wearily.

"That's not good enough! We'll lose her!" Jane caught her breath as a small amount of helplessness began to show through her face.

"Look, I don't see another choice!"

"How can we let her know that we want her to stay there?"

Diana was seemingly trying to wave to Jane. Jane put her arms up to show that she was okay.

"Chris, we have to be able to get to her! I would never forgive myself if we couldn't find her!"

"I know, I'm going to do the best I can!" It was plain to see that Chris had become the leader. Being the oldest and the one who knew the most, he was now feeling responsibility for Jane and Diana. Swallowing, he tried to think things through.

"Look, both of us have to get down! If I leave you and get Diana, we might not be able to find you again! Plus, I would feel safer if you were with me!" Chris screamed loudly to reach Jane's hearing range.

Jane stared hopelessly at Diana, her mind soaring back to the day when she first asked Diana to go with her. Jane stared with wide eyes at Diana, whispering, "I didn't know this could happen. I wouldn't have taken you if I had, you know that, right?"

"Jane, did you just say something?" Chris yelled.

Jane looked up sharply at Chris and hastily replied, "No, nothing!"

Both Jane and Chris had their parachutes caught on thick branches and were unable remove themselves from their location. Chris rummaged through his pockets and pulled out a pocketknife. Cutting himself out of his parachute he stepped from branch to branch and cut Jane free, too. Slowly, they began their decent. The going was onerous because the thickness of the vines was severely difficult to climb through. It took them almost an hour to reach the heavily laden undergrowth. At first Jane sat down, completely exhausted, and began to complain about her wrist. Chris climbed down by Jane and examined her wrist, determining that it was fine. Jane stood up, and holding her wrist in her other hand, she started to pull away the vegetation. Stumbling toward a mysterious huge hole that caught her attention, Jane kept a close eye on her continuously shifting surroundings. The hole looked like an endless abyss that someone or something had dug out. Never had Jane seen anything quite like it. It appeared to be on the edge of a small clearing where the vegetation had been smoothed out, and the hole looked big enough for Jane to crawl into.

"Wait!" Chris called out and Jane stopped.

"Chris, what's that?" Jane asked.

Once Chris caught up with Jane, he took stock of their surroundings. They were standing in a small clearing. There was a break in the pattern of trees, and the vegetation had been worn down.

The clearing was only about ten feet wide. Once again Jane turned and asked Chris, "What's that hole for?"

"I'm not sure. Might be for an animal."

"What kind of animal?" Jane asked, slightly nervous.

"A snake, maybe, or a gopher."

"Chris, what kind of a snake is that big and gophers don't live here! At least, I don't think they do," Jane said.

Jane's curiosity had gotten the better of her. She thought she had heard a noise come from inside but wasn't sure since there were tons of noises coming from every direction and a constant humming of insects. It was hard to make any noise stand out, and there wasn't any audible silence.

As Jane approached the hole, she could hear Diana saying in the back of her mind, "Come back, Jane, come back." But Jane didn't listen. She braced herself, took a deep breath and cautiously peered into the hole. Slightly bewildered, Jane stood back up and called to Chris, "There's nothing in there. Now what are we going to do about Diana?"

Reality can turn to dreams as events capture your every thought, but on occasion, a dream is a warning that your subconscious endeavors to present as vigilance. I have often wondered what powered these happenings. I know that when I created my plan, it grasped portions of dreams, but neither technique did I use.

Chapter 16

Heather had tried to contact the McTerms' home that morning, but hearing once more that neither Jane nor Diana were back, she began to worry intensely. Heather was also severely tired. A thousand sandbags were weighing down her whole body. She had spent the entire night awake. She told herself she would stay awake until Jane and Diana came back. It was morning now, and Heather was vividly tired. She was pulled down onto her couch by her shaky legs and instantaneously shut her eyes. "Just for a few minutes, then I'll get up," Heather whispered to herself, but she couldn't help the overwhelming drowsiness, and within a moment, she was asleep. A deep stir began to shift in her subconscious, and from the depths of the darkness, a dream slowly started to take shape.

Time began to rush backwards. Heather saw herself becoming younger, and soon she was just a small girl. Suddenly, everything came flooding back like a monstrous storm. She saw herself waving good-bye to her friend Jane and watched Jane walk home to her little house. Heather saw Jane's mom coming toward her with a flashlight. Once Jane was out of view, Heather turned around and went back inside. She saw herself laugh as her dad scooped her up and began carrying her upstairs. As her dad laid her in bed, she heard him say these words:

"Tomorrow is your birthday; you'll be six."

The voice echoed terribly all around Heather. She saw herself smile as she pulled her light pink bed sheets up to her chin and gave her dad a goodnight kiss. She watched herself fall asleep. Then, and only then, did she remember that dream, that dreaded dream from years ago. She began to relive it. She and Jane lost in an atrocious forest. Everywhere was green except for the small clearing that they were standing in. There was something right behind them; they had nowhere to run. They couldn't move, the vines tripped them and the moss, bushes and shrubs impaired their speed. Something was right behind them, chasing them! It would not let up. Like a bolt of lightning the dream disappeared, and Heather saw herself wake up and close that window. Close the window so the birds chirping would not be so loud. She saw herself wake up in the morning. She sat up and stretched. She watched as her mom came into her room and helped her down from the top bunk, even though she claimed she didn't need it. She watched her mom ask her that question that now Heather would never forget.

"So, did you have any dreams last night?"

Heather watched herself answer. She saw her lips move slowly as she replied, "No." The dream disappeared into the far outreaches of her imagination, and a sweet smile spread across her face as she remembered that it was her birthday.

Time started to move up again. Heather began to see the forest once more, except she was no longer small, she was seventeen again. At that time she heard the voice as it echoed around her, "You're running out of time; well, actually, you already have." The voice sniggered, "I can't believe that you still can't understand. I might just have to come out and tell you. I wasn't expecting this."

"Who are you! Please! Just tell me!" Heather said, gasping for breath.

"Who am I! I thought you knew that! Your imagination was so interesting and haunting, I knew I was going to use it. I love to twist around fate, though I had never become so involved before. Everything just spiraled out of control, and I grew attached to you, which was my biggest mistake!"

Heather yelled into the distance, a realization dawning on her, "You didn't want to send me with Jane. You knew what would happen! I knew I felt something among the breeze after my horse tripped over that root!"

The voice almost softly, almost normally, answered back, "I didn't want to let you go."

"But why?" Heather questioned.

Still in the less sinister tone, the voice answered back, "Listen very carefully. I don't know what I caused anymore. I know what I created, but it's like a chain reaction. To make it happen, certain events beforehand and after have been altered. All I did was watch until the day I realized that your life was to be doomed. Your imagination and mind was all so abnormal and exciting! I didn't mean to put *your* life in danger. Once I realized I had, I acted fast. Sort of panicked one might say." The voice grew quiet.

An icy chill burned around Heather; she didn't like it one bit. "I don't care if you like me! Can't you understand, I just want you to leave my friends and me alone! My life, I want it back! You have ruined everything! You give me a riddle and put that to decide my future! Why don't you just change things back?"

The voice returned to its high, abnormal, dark laugh. "You are the fool! You can't even understand the one thing that could have saved them, your very own friends! Now you are responsible," it growled, "I want you to remember that! Every day for the rest of your life! It is your fault!"

"Nothing is my fault! You just want someone else to blame!" Heather screamed, her confidence slipping away.

"I give you a chance to change things on your own. If you figure out my riddle it will lead to their safe return. Don't you understand, what's done is done! You could start a chain reaction of your own if you figure out my riddle, but I won't solve it for you! I don't want any more of this! I need to back out," the voice replied coldly.

Heather began panicking, but there was no one to hear. Finally, she tried to compose herself and yelled into the darkening forest, "Why is this my fault! And why can't you tell me who you are?"

"I have grown mellow over the years; ever since Eve bit that apple, I've felt that my work is done." The voice took a deep breath. "I come into people's conscience...no, imagination and see what I can find. If I find a very good imagination, I see if I can take bits of that and turn it into reality. Very clever, isn't it?" The voice began to disappear, and soon the forest.

Heather opened her eyes and began to sob. It was all so frustrating. "Why can't I just understand?" Heather asked herself, yelling harshly in her mind. "Understand what? That riddle or that none of this is real, just nightmares!"

Her mother entered the room, and not noticing her condition, began to cook breakfast.

"Mom, what's that?" Heather said, pointing to a section of the newspaper as she wiped away the tears from her face.

"It's the answers to last weeks crossword puzzle. Why do you ask, dear?"

Heather drew in a sharp breath. The realization of something had just dawned on her.

She ran upstairs to her room as fast as her legs would allow her. She rustled through some papers until she came in contact with one of the several copies. Pulling out her chair she sat down at her desk. She laid the paper down flat and began to read it softly:

"Some have been told
As this story will unfold
Made from crooks
Your friends will suffer
But you already know this
From no other."

Heather decided to try and make sense of the poem first. She reread the last two lines and stared hard at them as they finally began to make sense. She always wondered about the last two lines. "But you already know this from no other" had made no sense to Heather, but now she understood. She now saw that "from no other" meant from "no one else." She, *she* knew. Heather sat back in her chair as she remembered the dream. She knew about the dream about being chased by something, some monster. "But what does that have to do with Jane?" she asked herself. She had seen Jane in the forest. "If this dream is a true picture of reality, then that means that Jane is being faced with something horrid." Heather shivered.

"I, I should be there," Heather said slowly. She didn't know if she could believe that the poem told about the future, but she decided to try her idea, the whole reason she had decided to take out the poem in the first place. She picked up a pen and began to circle worlds like in a crossword puzzle. As she did this she began to talk to herself about what word or words she might be looking for.

"In my last dream," she sniffed, "nightmare, I discovered many disturbing things that I'd forgotten, but I still don't know what I'm looking for. To change what's happening I need something that can affect Jane and the trial. Think hard, Heather, what about the case, the trial. Something, anything." After awhile she had to stop. "I just don't get it," she murmured as she slammed her pen onto her desk.

The sky is blue
The grass is green
The sun is yellow
But when we sit on the grass
Looking up at the sky
Staring at the setting sun
All we see is tranquility.

Chapter 17

Chris cried out in agony as he painfully caught his leg on a branch. How long had it been, hours upon hours, or not nearly as much? Chris couldn't tell and neither could Jane. They had been pushing through the dense, thick foliage moving only inches at a time. The air was thick, it was hard to breath and every second made your heart jump. Unidentifiable shapes would rush past them or scurry overhead. The going was nearly impossible, and by now they weren't even sure if they were headed in the right direction.

"Chris, shouldn't we be there by now?"

"Jane, I don't know what to tell you. I mean, we can't see a foot in front of us."

Jane had to admit that was true, and Chris was doing the best he could. Everything was so compressed together. The vines and undergrowth covered everything like a heavy blanket you couldn't get out of. They had to shove, rip and pull their way through every step.

"What if we got turned and were headed in the opposite direction?" Jane asked, looking for reassurance.

"I was starting to think that myself," Chris replied.

Wrong answer.

"That's it! Stay here! I'm going to climb that tree and see where we are."

"You can't climb that! It's at least a hundred feet! Plus, I don't want you leaving my sight."

Jane's eyes blazed an upset panicked stare, and her voice almost trembled as she uttered softly, "Then it seems that you'll have to come with me."

Chris stared back at Jane and decided that it was a better idea than what they were doing, so he obliged.

This task was much more laborious than Jane had imagined. Her arms and legs had grown weak, and after they had gotten about halfway up, she collapsed onto a nearby branch.

"Are you okay, Jane?" Chris called out from above.

"I feel like I can't move one more inch."

"I'll keep going as long as I can see you sitting there."

"Don't worry, I'm not moving."

Chris closed his eyes for a moment then reopened them as he stared upward. Talking more to himself than Jane, he stated, "I'll be fine. Not that much more left."

Jane didn't answer as she looked upward at the forty or so feet that seemed to be left.

The sun had slightly started to dip downward but still as bright as it had been. The trees almost completely blocked the sun's blazing light, and the jungle took on a darkened hue. Jane could hardly make out its rays as she tried to follow Chris's moves while he climbed steadily upward. By now he was a small figure high above her.

Jane listened intently to the surrounding sounds. She thought she heard Chris yelling, but it was impossible to tell for sure. Jane watched as the figure seemed to start moving downward. Jane waited as patiently as she could while he climbed down. Once he had reached her, she anxiously awaited his news.

"Start climbing down, and hurry."

Jane looked at him for a moment as he passed by her. Noticing the tone in his voice, she came to the conclusion that they weren't in any danger. Taking in a deep breath, she followed Chris. She tried feverishly to get information out of him on the climb down. "Did you see Diana; is she okay?"

"Stop taking, just listen."

"What am I listening for?"

"Be quiet!"

"Just tell if Diana's still alright."

"I'll tell you everything in a minute, and yeah, I think she's okay."

Jane felt a wave of emotion roll over her like nothing she had ever felt. A smile spread across her face even though a big part of her didn't understand why. After they had reached the bottom, Jane knew enough to stay silent. Chris had been a calm, cheerful guy when she first met him even though he was very sturdy and tough. He wasn't the type to waste time, so if he wanted to stand still and stare, Jane decided she would too. A few moments later, Jane heard a loud bang. It sounded muffled, but it was undeniable. Chris turned to face the direction it seemed to come from.

"I can tell you what's happening, but we only have five minutes, so listen."

Jane stared about to burst.

"When I got to the top I immediately located Dana..."

"Diana," Jane corrected.

"Sorry, Diana. It's a good thing we stopped when we did because we were beginning to go off to the left. Diana is only about twenty-five feet away. In that direction," Chris said, pointing in the direction the bang had come from. "I could yell to her and I came up with an idea. I was on guard duty when this happened and I had my gun which was on my belt. I undid it and threw it to her. Luckily, very luckily she caught it. Next, my watch. I had two. One on my wrist and one pinned to my uniform. I would always wear that watch, but I'd never use it. I guess it finally..."

Jane stared hard at Chris, an exasperated look on her face, "Anyway," Chris hurried, "I gave one to Diana and..."

"She caught that, too? She can't catch anything," Jane interrupted again.

"Well, I guess she knew she had to. We are very lucky that they're still intact. The watch that was on my uniform had its glass smashed, but still works. I told her after thirdly minutes to shoot the first shot.

Then, for every ten minutes shoot another one and that we would try and follow it."

Jane looked slightly surprised. She felt that it was a very clever idea.

"She should shoot another one in about three minutes so listen."

They heard the second shot. It just barely rose above the insane chatter that swirled around them. Following it as fast as they could, they pulled apart the shrubs and vines as they pressed on. Then the third shot came, still they ran onward. It was the third shot that sent a tugging at Jane's heart. It came from right above them. Looking up, Jane thought she could just barely make out the colored parachute.

Chris lifted up his pant leg and pulled out another gun.

"How many of those do you have?" Jane said, taking a step back.

"Just two. We always have two."

"Wouldn't the two lawyers, Tom and, ah, Joe have taken them?"

"Those two?" Chris said with a laugh as he held the gun up to the canopy. "They can't do anything right." Turning the gun away from the parachute, Chris fired one shot. It was resounding and many shapes scampered away.

"Is she hurt, can she get down by herself?"

"She said she was fine except for some cuts and aches. She asked me to just wait down here."

"If she could get down, why didn't she do it before?"

"I don't know." Chris looked at Jane and gave a small grin. "Maybe you should ask her yourself when she gets down."

It was near impossible for Jane to imagine, but she had never felt this way before. A soft lump of weariness hung in Jane's throat, and she felt a blanket of courageousness sweep over her, for she, in some form, had saved her friend. Jane never knew that she would try to climb a hundred-foot tree for Diana or wander deep into a dense jungle. She felt very horrified and hopeless, but getting Diana back took some of that away.

The going was slow for Diana, and after awhile Jane sat on the loamy earth and watched wearily. Finally, she was no more than thirty feet up, and Jane couldn't wait to see her face again. She was gravely worried and wanted everything to be over now. Diana continued her decent and dropped from the massive tree when she was about ten feet up. Landing right in front of Jane, she gave out onto the vine-covered floor.

Standing up, Jane tried to assist Diana as she said, overcome with joy, "You're okay! Diana, I was so…"

"I still am."

"Am what?

"Scared." Diana lay on the ground breathing in long gasps of the thick air.

Jane hadn't planned that far ahead. "Now, we are together." Jane thought, "But what are we suppose to do?"

Diana voiced aloud what Jane had been thinking, "What do we do now?"

By reflex they both turned to stare at Chris. He spoke slowly as if already knowing he was the one to answer this. "I had completely forgotten about my watches until just earlier. I estimated that Jane and I spent three hours finding you, plus an extra two hours climbing up and down that tree. Then it took you, Diana, about an hour to get down. I think that we got here at about ten in the morning. It's four thirty now. My best idea is not to stay here. There's nowhere to move or think."

"We can't just leave!" Jane added loudly.

"That's not what I meant. I think we should go back to the area Jane and I landed in. There was a small, flat space where we could all sleep, and because we have a pathway that we cut out, it would only take an hour or so."

Jane and Diana stood for a moment, tired and exhausted. They knew that staying where they were wasn't a good idea and that going back to a place that Jane was already familiar with would somehow be better.

Taking one last look upward, they retreated back the way they had come. The going was fairly easy because Jane and Chris had already cleared a path. In just over an hour and a half, they came back to the same spot they had been many hours earlier. Chris looked upward, observing the fact that it was approaching night.

"We better be careful because several animals are nocturnal and hunt at night."

"What exactly is that suggesting?"

Interrupting Jane and Chris, Diana asked, "What's that?" as she pointed to the edge of the smoothed-out area.

"Oh, it's just some hole. I looked at it before and nothing was there."

"Really?"

"Yeah, come here and I'll show you." Jane motioned to Diana.

Jane knelt down beside the hole and put her head slightly inside. Pulling it back out, she raised her stare to the bushes just in front of her and found herself staring into two ruthless, shining black eyes.

Jane gave a high-pitched scream as she pulled her face away from the underbrush. She ran back over to where Diana and Chris were standing and started to shiver. She tried to tell them what she had seen. "There is something behind that bush! It has huge black eyes!"

"We have to get out of here," Diana said, visibly frightened.

"We do not. It's probably just a snake," Chris stated as he stared upward, trying to make out the fading sun through the dense canopy. "And if you're afraid of one snake then I don't know how long you're gonna last in here."

"Chris, don't say stuff like that," Diana whined. Turning slightly, she stared directly over Jane's shoulder. She began to stammer with her eyes fixated on the same spot. "Jane, how big wwwas the snake supposed to be?"

"Well, I don't know. Not too big, I guess."

"How big is too big?"

Before Jane could answer, Diana screamed and pointed for Jane and Chris to turn around.

Jane swallowed hard. She wasn't sure if she wanted to see what was lurking behind her. She could hear the snake's slithering getting louder and louder. Almost at once, Chris and Jane whirled around to see what Diana was gaping at. Jane almost fainted! It was the most hideous thing they had ever seen in their whole life! Jane had a slight flashback of home and school. She saw herself peering into another classroom and seeing a poster of some kind of huge snake. Too filled with fear, she brushed the thought out of her mind. The snake looked more like a monster than a normal serpent. It was as big around as a beach ball and donned thick black scales. Its eyes were round like sinister, pitch-black marbles. The eyes swirled their blackish color as they stared unblinking, dead as night. It looked as though they could hypnotize Jane on the spot. The snakes tongue flickered in and out as it moved steadily forward, but its width was nearly forgotten when they saw the length of it. That's what kept Jane, Diana and Chris rooted to the spot. The snake's body was like nothing they had ever seen before. It continued sliding out from behind the underbrush. First it was five feet, then ten, now around twenty. It was a colossal mess of coils. Steadily advancing forward, it came closer to its prey.

"Ah, well, this is, is a, ah, not what I was thinking of," Chris said nervously.

"We should get out of here. 'We do not, it's just a snake'," Jane said, mimicking Chris's voice.

Chris glared at Jane. "Look, we have to leave, now."

"You mean run for it?" Diana asked.

"We can't try to climb a tree it would get us in a second."

"I'm scared," Diana whimpered.

"We've been running all day! I don't want to run anymore! I already climbed a tree, I've already done all that! I just want to lay down." Jane had a look of desperate lassitude. Despite her exhaustion, terror gripped her heart, making a chilling fear well inside her. She stood frozen to the grassy earth, staring at the snake's unblinking eyes. She tried to rip her gaze away but couldn't.

Chris began to speak. "My best guess is that this is an anaconda."

"Like that matters now," Diana said to herself.

"It does. Anacondas aren't that fast on land," Chris added.

With all her might, Jane torn her eyes away from the anaconda's stare and muttered, "On three."

Chris whispered, "One. Two. Three."

Jane took off with all the might that was left in her. The huge snake had blocked off their only path, so they began blindly pushing their way through the vines, moss, and undergrowth. Branches whipped her face has she pounded her legs upon the ground. The going felt so slow, and every move took clawing and pushing; it felt like she was running through mud that was up to her chin. As she looked behind her, a crash sounded in her head as she saw that the anaconda had started to chase them.

"It's right behind us!" Chris yelled.

Jane didn't know what to do. She was running fast, but how long could she keep that up? The undergrowth was so thick that you could barely breathe. It was almost impossible to keep up a fast pace. Moss, brushes, trees, and branches were everywhere. Jane started thinking, "What if I don't make it back to New York, and they will never know the truth? They will never find me. Never." That scared Jane. It made her feel so small and helpless. She could hear Diana slightly behind her gasping for breath. Chris was in front of Jane but had pulled back. The only thing that kept Jane going was the thought of a thirty-foot snake right behind them.

Then the inevitable happened; Diana tripped.

"Get up, Diana!" Jane screamed. "Diana, you must hurry!!" Jane's voice was a shrill, high-pitched panic.

Diana was too winded. She was hurting all over and had a gouge on her forehead. Blood was running over her face, mixing with tears, blinding her vision. It only took a moment for the anaconda to surround them. Diana couldn't see its face. It engulfed them. Jane hurriedly helped Diana up. All three stood together as the anaconda started to squeeze. Diana felt sharp pains in her stomach as the snake's grip tightened. Her face was turning a grayish purple from lack of air. The anaconda pulled unmercifully and harder with every second. Blood fell from Diana's deep cut forehead onto the anaconda's long, scaly back. Curling her hand into a fist with all her might, she began to pound on the anaconda's back, causing it to stop squeezing momentarily. It turned its long scaly head toward Diana, its long, blood red tongue slithering in and out of its mouth. Jane took this chance to reach up and grab an overhanging vine. With the last of her energy she swung it over the anaconda's head. Tying it into a knot, she pulled the vine with all her might. Chris picked up a fallen branch and slammed it down onto the anaconda's head. It fell senseless to the ground.

Jane, Chris and Diana collapsed onto the anaconda, taking in long gasps of air. Sweat dripped down their faces as the thick heat added to their discomfort. Shaking, Jane tried to stand up, but still too weak, she fell back onto the anaconda and shivered. All she wanted to do was get off of this gigantic scaly thing. Looking around for something to help her up, she saw that all around her were thick vines and moss hanging down from the tree branches. Brightly colored flowers decorated the undergrowth, seeming incredibly beautiful. Jane would never have expected pain and misery to come from a place like this.

Jane finally ventured to speak. Her voice was hoarse and raspy. "I can't take it all in. I'm standing in the Amazon in the middle of an anaconda, and all we wanted to do was get that picture to the court."

"All *you* wanted..." Jane thought she heard Chris mumble.

"Jane, where's the picture?" Diana said weakly.

A look of panic crossed Jane's face, which quickly vanished and was replaced with a sigh of relief.

"Here it is. It was in my pocket, the one with a zipper." Jane coughed harshly. "I put it there before we parachuted into our own nightmares."

Diana looked like she was going to pass out at any moment. Feebly, she wiped blood from her face. "I must look just horrible!" she said, trying to force a smile.

Jane had to look away as Diana wiped away more blood from the exposed gouge.

"That bad, huh?" Diana whispered.

Jane looked back at Diana, but it was hard to. You could tell that she was in a vast amount of pain.

"Diana, you gonna be okay?" Jane had to stop and catch her breath. "I mean, it looks pretty painful. We have to stop the bleeding."

"I guess I'll be all right, but it hurts real bad. Jane, maybe Chris has something we could use to stop the bleeding," Diana said as she held her hand up to the gash.

"Diana, how is Chris?" Jane asked because she could not see his face.

"Chris is fine," he mumbled as he sat up.

"Chris, what should we do about Diana's forehead? She's losing a lot of blood."

"Here, take this," Chris said as he handed Diana a white handkerchief that he removed from his pocket. "I don't care if it gets dirty." Chris didn't even look up. He stared blankly at the ground.

Diana smiled, then winced as she put the handkerchief on her forehead.

"We better get moving before this anaconda wakes up," Diana said, standing up.

Jane wasn't sure how to physically get over the snake; it was everywhere, and stepping on it wasn't too appealing. Diana tried to jump over it and almost made it. She quickly stepped off the anaconda and waited for the others. Once they were over it they began to move as quickly as their legs would allow them.

Jane looked upward often. She was trying to make out the sky, but it had become impossible. The trees took up most of the view, but then there were the bushes and branches that carpeted every open space. The moss and vines hung from overhead, adding to the condensed jungle. All Jane could see was green, and it was impossible to think. There was a strong constant humming of insects, a humming that filled her head and left no room for logical thought. Jane tried to cover her eyes and ears so that she could get a moment's silence, but the humming was too strong. It engulfed her.

"I want to get out of here," Jane whined pitifully. She almost had to yell.

"None of us want to stay here, Jane," Chris replied.

The going became harder and harder. Each step was a weighed-down effort. Their breathing was long and pressured because of the density of their surroundings and the thickness in the air. Suddenly as Jane crushed a dead leaf that lay in her path, something devastating started to happen: the little light that made it through the canopy totally disappeared, while faint raindrops began to fall upon their heads.

"Oh, no. It's going to be night soon," Jane groaned.

"It is night," Chris commented on Jane's statement.

"We have to sleep out here?" Diana sounded sort of surprised and disgusted.

"Unless you see an alternative," Chris said sharply.

Walking a little farther, they came to a large tree with vines spreading everywhere. The long, bulky vines seemed to cover the tree completely, twisting and overlapping the whole way up. They were as thick as the branches on the tree and they grew long green leaves. The tree itself was abnormally huge. It was the biggest tree that any of them had ever witnessed. Being about thirty feet around, it had roots coming out of the ground that were almost as tall as Jane. Jane couldn't even see the top of the tree since it disappeared into the green mist from far above.

"We'll sleep here. Go under the roots and vines to help stay dry. I can't think of a better idea, so hurry up before it starts pouring and you really get soaked," Chris commanded.

"How's your head?" Jane asked Diana as she saw her wince.

"I've never experienced more pain in my life," Diana replied as she moved the handkerchief away from her forehead. It was a ghastly sight. Almost all the skin that covered her forehead had been torn away, leaving red blood smeared through her hair. Only a small portion in the center of her forehead was very deep, and that's what kept her from bleeding continuously. Diana winced again as small droplets of rain fell onto her wound. Carefully placing the blood-soaked cloth back onto her head, she began to try and get underneath one of the roots.

"What if that thing comes back?" Jane shivered.

"Just don't talk about that now. All we need to worry about now is getting a good night's rest," Chris answered.

As high above as the moon was, it still shone down to provide what little light it could on the darkening jungle.

Every lie holds a lie that can't be proven.

Chapter 18

The hot blinding sun shone over the heads of two criminals, thieves, two masters in disguise. They stumbled over a huge hill with nothing but sand behind them. Looking up, their tired, dreary eyes sparkled with delight as they saw the makings of a town in front of them. The town looked large but rather poor. All the houses in their view looked small, and there weren't any huge offices or hotels towering above. It looked like a small, peaceful town, but to Tom and Joe, who were used to big offices and New York City, this place was Nowheresville.

"How far do you think we are from New York?"

"I have no clue. Why would you think I'd know!" Tom snapped back.

Joe hastily tried to keep pace with Tom. "No need to yell, hey, I'm gettin' edgy myself. Things weren't supposed to go like this. Never did we figure this into our plan. I just hope those girls crashed somewhere no one will ever find them."

Tom shot a backwards glance at Joe, his eyes blazing. "That's not half the reason why I'm 'edgy'. I've never been more tired or thirsty or hungry in my whole damn life! Never! Now, let's hurry up and get into that town before I pass out!"

Joe looked at the tortuously scorching sand as a moment's silence lapsed. Throwing a glance at Tom, he voiced, "What are we goin' to tell...the world? The trial was big enough, but what about us and two girls disappearing?"

"Don't forget about Chris," Tom sighed.

"Oh, yeah. Man, we are in deep..."

"Shut up for a minute, will ya! Stop babbling!" Tom yelled, shoving Joe sideways. "Do I have to do all the thinking around here? Before we enter that town, we better have a flawless plan because we have worked to hard to get found out by this!"

Tom and Joe stopped walking for a moment and stared at each other. They were so exhausted and tired that even trying to think up something logical seemed nearly impossible. They stumbled down the hill in search of a plan.

Once they reached the outskirts of the town, they began to look for the nearest house. They passed by many small stores before they found one. It was small like the rest but had a comfortable, friendly look with small, round hedges and flowers lining the walkway. It donned small windows with lacy drapes covering them. Once Tom and Joe reached the door, Tom took the liberty to ring the doorbell. They had to wait some time before a noise sounded from within. When the door opened, they were faced with a lady that looked to be in her late thirties. Her petite figure accented the seemingly natural dirty blonde hair that fell just passed her shoulders. Even though she was so small, she claimed a distinguished voice. It was sharp but sweet.

"You fellas look just awful. What happened to you?" the woman said cautiously.

"Well, miss, we've, ah, have to make a phone call," Tom said.

"I don't like people who don't answer my questions."

"Sorry, miss..."

"It's Rachell."

"Okay, sorry, Rachell. We got lost and have been walkin' through that desert thing," Joe said, pointing.

"How, why would you be walking through that?" the lady replied as she looked in the direction of Joe's gaze.

"Look, can we explain later? We need water, please," Tom said pleadingly.

Seeing how much in need they really were, she let them come inside. After giving them water and what little food she found in her cupboard, she showed them to her phone.

"I'll be upstairs getting something, so you two," she paused, "gentlemen behave."

After she had disappeared up her hard oak stairs, Tom begin to dial.

"Hello, you have reached the New York court..."

"Yes, could you please put one of the police, or preferably police officer Barry Lonad, on the phone. This is Tom Hankar and Joe Tremmer."

"Oh, yes, of course, hold on, please." You could hear the surprise in her voice as she put down the phone and ran to get Barry Lonad.

While they were waiting, Tom snapped at Joe, "From now on, I do the talking! All you do is mess things up! You didn't have to tell her we came from that desert! Now we can't anyone anything different!" Hot anger was exploding from Tom's voice.

Before Joe could answer, Tom began to converse on the phone.

Barry sounded rather shocked. "Tom, is it really you?" Barry said hopefully.

"Of course it's us."

"We've been looking for you. It's been all over the news. Are you guys alright? What happened, and by the way, where are you?"

"We don't know, hold on a sec." Tom put down the phone and yelled up the stairs, "Excuse me, miss, er, Rachell where are we?"

At first there was no reply, but then a girl showed up at the top of the stairs. She looked about sixteen. When she spoke she had the same tone as her mother. "You're in Sanderson, Texas. How could you not have known that? I ain't one to ask questions, but what are your names?"

"I'm Tom Hankar and this is Joe Tremmer," Tom answered hastily, eager to be back on the phone.

Turning around, Tom picked up the phone and continued

conversing with Barry. "We're in Sanderson, Texas."

"How the hell did you end up in Texas?"

"It's a long story, but right now we're in Texas and we want to leave."

"You just sit tight and we'll send someone down to pick you guys up. I guess we'll have to use a private jet. Why don't you guys put someone on the phone that can give us the name of the nearest airport."

"Sure, one moment," Tom said as Rachell came back down the stairs.

"Rachell, could you please get on the phone and talk to the police officer? He has some questions he'd like to ask you."

"I suppose so," Rachell answered as she took the phone from Tom.

"Hello, this is Barry Lonad. Could you tell me where the nearest airport is?"

As she conversed, the girl that had been at the top of the stairs was now standing in front of Tom and Joe. She spoke as if she knew something. It gave Tom and Joe an eerie feeling. Her voice was soft, slow and steady. "You guys picked this house out of the whole of Texas."

"What do you mean by that?" Joe asked.

"I mean, I know your secret."

Joe looked at Tom in bewilderment. Joe whispered to Tom, "How could she know! She lives in Texas! Who could have told her?"

"She must be talking about something else," Tom answered in a violent, hushed tone.

"You're right. I mean, it's got to be something else," Joe replied as he turned back toward the girl.

"Look, I don't have any way of provin'..." She paused as if rethinking. "I might hold my silence if you tell me exactly where Jane is."

"Who?" Tom said, puzzled.

"You know, the girl you kidnapped?"

A swift slap seemed to hit Tom in the face and a chill ran down his back. "You must have us confused with someone else," he stammered.

"Oh, believe me, I don't. She told me everything. She told me everything right before she left on her way to New York. She said she was taking a friend. The next thing I know, you and two girls are missing. Now you're back. So where are they?"

Tom gulped, "Look, I don't know where your friend is, alright?"

"Liar," the girl said with a cold, slim smile.

Tom could have turned to stone right then and there.

"Well, that's done," Rachell said with a sigh.

"What should we do?" Joe asked nervously.

"Oh, yeah. They told me to bring you guys to a hotel, but I told them that I wouldn't hear of it. Even though you are strangers, you seem harmless enough. You'll be staying with me and my daughter tonight."

"You didn't have to do that," Tom said grimly.

"I wouldn't have it any other way. Now, follow me. I'll show you to our guest room and the shower."

Reluctantly, they followed.

"Ah, Rachell?" Tom said as he headed up the stairs.

"Yes."

"What's your daughter's name?"

"How silly of me," Rachell said as if she had completely forgotten to introduce them. Halfway up the stairs, she turned and said, "Tom, Joe, this is my daughter, Leea."

Leea looked back at them with an odd glint in her eyes.

The breaking point. Everyone hits it eventually but is forced to get back up. It is those of us who shatter who truly fail.

Chapter 19

The entire McTerm family was devastated over the confirmation of two young girls disappearing. Even though the police could not confirm that Jane and Diana were the two missing girls, the odds were too high. Mrs. McTerm was hardly consolable and spent her time staring blankly at the television news. She was the most heart-wrenched out of everyone. Jake, Mark and Mike were becoming exceedingly worried about her mental health, so they decided to invite Heather and her mom over for dinner. Once they arrived, she did in fact rise from her chair and converse with them. Heather was still on crutches and hobbled around the house. Her ankle was almost healed, but it was a constant reminder to Heather that her accident was the last memory she had with Jane. As they picked uncomfortably at their meal, it was hard to keep the conversation going without bringing up Jane. After the meal was over, Heather and her mom went into the family room accompanied by Mrs. McTerm. They switched on the television and began to watch the news.

"Hello, and welcome to the news at ten. One of our top stories today is: an unidentified plane disturbingly crashed somewhere over the northwest part of South America several hours earlier today. The cause is unknown and there is still no word of passengers..."

Mrs. McTerm turned the television off and settled back into her chair. She held a deep, distressed, desolate look in her eyes, like a part of her was missing. It seemed as though she was going to just sit there and blindly stare at the blank TV, but eventually she turned her head, voicing her thoughts.

"I just can't bear to watch the news anymore. I'm so afraid that Jane and Diana will..." She swallowed. "Do you think their...?" Mrs. McTerm couldn't finish her sentence.

"How could you imply such a thing, Mrs. McTerm? I'm sure they're fine," Heather said, trying to dismiss her dreams.

"I never thought a day like this would come. I just wish she'd come home."

"Oh, I don't know what to say. We all feel so terrible. Jane and Diana were like family to us. We'll say a prayer for them," Heather's mom added, concerned.

"How's your ankle?" Mrs. McTerm voiced suddenly.

"Um," Heather said, surprised, "it's getting better. Don't worry about it. I won't need crutches in about a week."

"Two weeks," Heather's mom corrected her.

They continued their conversation well into the night. It wasn't until nearly 12:30 a.m. that Heather and her mother finally exited the house. Mrs. McTerm said good-bye and goodnight quietly as they walked to their car.

On their way home, Heather spoke softly, "Mom, I'm scared."

"Why, honey?"

"I never really believed in my dreams; well, I never really wanted to, but now..."

"But now what, dear?" Heather's mom said as she made a right turn, a tinge of exasperation in her voice.

"Now, I'm afraid that they're real."

"Honey, I thought we had already discussed this."

"Mom, think about it. Every night it's something, and it all seems to make more sense by each day. I still can't quite piece everything together, but I know there's truth to my dreams; it's all too uncanny."

"Like what?"

"I can't quite say yet. I'm just scared."

"All right, Heather. You still don't make much sense to me, though."

As they pulled into Heather's driveway, the stars sparkled through the empty air. A soft breeze glided across the sky, splashing through the trees on its way through the inky darkness. The grass blew in different directions as grasshoppers descended from the long stalks. A soft hum carried along the vitreous breeze. It was barely audible, but was there for all who cared to listen. As Heather exited the car, she heard the soft hum as it fell past her. Her mom held the front door open for her, and as she entered her house, she became vividly tired. Making her way upstairs, she tried to blink away the sleep that was creeping up on her, but it was impossible. Within five minutes she was fast asleep.

Blurring colors appeared, and for the first time in all of Heather's dreams, it became bright. Grass gradually started to appear, and radiant resplendent trees with white buds were everywhere. A shiny sun shone, lighting everything with a wonderful glow. The more Heather stared at the scene, the more she realized that things were missing. She wasn't seeing the whole picture, but it was all so enchanting that she didn't really care. Heather was standing on the luscious grass looking at something, but she saw nothing. Suddenly, her mind turned on this place, for it gave her the worst feeling out of any other dream. It gave her a feeling in the pit of her stomach that made her eyes burn. She gazed upward and saw a single white rose lying in front of her, just a few feet ahead. It was the most perfectly exquisite thing she had ever seen. Each pedal was a blinding white with impeccable shape. The green stem was just the right length with small thorns balanced ideally on it. The flower stood out from everything else so much that the entire landscape started to deteriorate, and soon nothing but the white rose stayed visible. Heather began to see the more familiar dark, blurred colors, and the sky was replaced with a dark, haunting black.

Her surroundings were incongruous, but they seemed like nothing to Heather as she waited for the other part of her dream to come. As ready as Heather was, this still made her shiver and frightened her beyond anything else.

"Do you like my present?" the voice said in a hushed tone.

"It's so perfect. What is it for?" Heather asked. She could not tear her eyes from the rose. It was too bright, too white, and too perfect.

"It was the least I could do."

"I don't understand."

"You never understand! You are worthless!"

"Why would you give me a rose? Can't this just be over! I want this all to go away."

"The rose isn't for you, and sorry, but no. You chose this, remember? You're the one that couldn't figure out my words."

"But I came close. I know I'm getting closer," Heather said, uncertain.

"Well, I can't say because that would take the fun out of it." The voice laughed; it sounded more like a harsh hissing noise.

"Oh, please!" Heather said, summing up her courage. "You're just too afraid and too full of guilt to get more involved! You said it yourself, didn't you? You're scared that if you do any more, this reality will become even more insane! Now, why can't you just tell me? It's already too late according to you."

The voice sighed, then answered, "Think about it! My proposal is not to tell you answers to the past or future. You pick what happens to you; therefore, you must find things out on your own. The future will tell you if you are right. Answer me this, do you like my present?"

Heather looked at the white rose; it gave her the most uneasy feeling.

"It's so flawless that it's, it's ugly, hideous. It seems…so evil."

Heather heard the voice's laugh fade away, and she was left with the rose. The rose frightened her so much that it was as if she knew that it brought a dreadful feeling with it. She tried to wake up, she tried to run away from it, she even tried to call for the voice to come back, but nothing happened. The rose burned into Heather's memory. It disappeared, and Heather's eyes flickered opened. Sitting up, she tried to blink away the memories. She now dreaded each day because she knew that after the day comes night. Heather lay back down and looked out her window envying the unwavering stars, hoping tomorrow would never come.

Dark gray clouds were all that you could make out through the stormy atmosphere. A gloomy, desolate mood hung above the saturnine sky. The vast trees were soaked, and mud was churned up everywhere. Loud howls could be heard, and other loud cries were coming from all directions.

Jane tried to get as hidden from view as possible. Feeling so small, she stayed huddled under a tree root waiting for the others to wake up.

"Jane, are you awake?" Diana asked in a whisper.

"Yeah, I was hoping that this was a dream and I'd wake up at home." Jane sighed and leaned against the tree.

"What are we supposed to do? How to we get out of this place?" Diana asked, half-hoping for an answer.

"Diana, we're never leaving; we're all going to die out here."

"Don't say that. It's very discouraging," Chris said, opening his eyes.

"Well, it's true!" Jane yelled back as tears started to well up in her eyes.

"Listen, if you're going to act like that, then just leave! I need as much logical thought from the two of you as possible. I don't know what to do or how to get out of here, but you're not really helping by saying that we're all going to die," Chris said in a sober but commanding tone.

"Sorry," Jane mumbled.

Chris stood up and helped Jane up. Diana tried to stand up by herself but couldn't. She had become very weak after losing all that blood.

"Diana, are you okay?" Chris said, eyeing her carefully.

"I guess so, I mean, there's nothing much I can do." Diana pressed the handkerchief against her forehead. She was still hard to look at, and the handkerchief was now completely stained with a dark red.

"Where should we go?" Chris asked, looking for a suggestion as he tried to drink some of the oncoming raindrops.

"What's the point in going anywhere? We should just stay here. Think about it. We don't know what direction we're going, it's raining, and we're lost."

"We should go back to where we landed. There must be something in our parachutes, a rope, a flare, something that we can use to radio back. Anything," Diana said hopefully.

"You want to go back to that snake's home!" Jane said shrilly.

"Sshhhh. Be quiet," Chris said in a voice that made Jane shiver, a voice that Jane had heard before when she had to be silent.

"Why?" Diana whispered.

"Do not move or scream; it might not see us," Chris said, still looking behind the two girls.

"What is it!" Jane whispered in a frightened voice.

"Just a big cat," he said, more talking to himself than Jane.

"Oh God help us, oh no, oh no," Diana repeated to herself quietly.

Jane slowly turned around; she could hear her feet move across the mud. She looked up at what appeared to be a jaguar. It was walking, not toward them, but like it was passing by. Its low growl could be heard through the rain. The heavy raindrops ran down its thick coat. As it turned its head, it stared directly into Jane's eyes. It stopped and stared. Jane saw the red bloodstain around the jaguar's mouth, she almost yelled in relief. The jaguar turned and kept on walking, not amused by the strange figures in its territory.

"That was lucky," Chris said softly.

"H, how come it, w, walked away, like that?" Diana asked, visibly shaken.

"Didn't you see the blood on its face? It had just eaten. I guess it wasn't in the mood to..."

"Eat us!" Diana interrupted bitterly. Chris glared at her but said nothing.

"I've never seen a jaguar up close and free like that," Jane added, almost in awe.

For a moment they stood quiet. Listening to the raindrops, the shrill noises of far-off animals, the constant hum and the silence. The silence that was always there, surrounding them but never showing.

"What now is full is later empty," Chris said, looking at Diana and Jane.

"What does that mean?" Jane asked, herself feeling a thousand watchful eyes peering at her from all directions.

"You know what I mean," Chris answered as he saw the color drain from Jane's face.

"Let's get moving," Diana whispered.

Walking became too hard as the thickness of the undergrowth became impossible to move through. It was everywhere and you couldn't see anything but the green plants and vines.

"I'm starving," Diana stated.

"We all are," Chris replied, then added, "I have an idea."

"An idea! How can you get an idea? There's nowhere to go. There's nothing to think up; we have no options!" Jane said. The frustration was plainly written on her face.

"All I'm saying is common sense. If we go this way it's much harder than that way," Chris said, pointing his fingers. "If you think about it, that means that the harder way has been traveled the least, if at all, and the other way has been traveled much more."

"You mean, if we go the easier way we might find some form of civilization?" Jane said excitedly.

"That's the best we can do for now," Chris said, turning around, not quite answering Jane's question.

The going was much faster, and soon they came back to where they had landed. Quickly they passed it, not wanting to run into *anything*. After a few hours they decided to stop and rest. The sun had just started to come out, and it could now be detected through the canopy. They sat for a while trying to build up enough strength to keep going.

"Hey, look!" Diana said, pointing to a nearby bush. There were some small animals eating berries off it.

"Yes, food," Chris said, standing up.

"How do you know we can eat it?" Jane asked.

"Jane, if the animals can eat it, then we can," Diana said as she walked over to the bush. The trio then began to eat hungrily, robbing the bush of all its berries.

Once they had finished the sun was just beginning to sink leaving a dark shadow.

"Not night again," Diana muttered to herself.

"Do you hear something?" Chris asked.

"Of course I hear things; this place never shuts up!" Jane said, putting her hands over her ears.

"No, I mean, do you hear something just beyond that bush?" Chris said, as a slow chill coursed its way down Jane's sweat-drenched back. Jane's heart froze. Diana turned her head; cold fear was shining in her eyes. A low growl could be heard, but its body could not be placed.

"Oh God, where is it?" Diana whispered urgently. They could hardly see as the light gave way to inky blackness.

"I don't know, I don't know," Jane answered back.

There was a rustle in the leaves behind them, but then it was gone. The sun's diminutive light was now replaced with a deep, dark blanket that suffocated all helpful light.

"What do we do?" Jane said, looking at Chris.

"I, I don't know," Chris replied.

After sensing the fear in Chris's tone, Jane lost all courage. Staring helplessly at the scene around her, she could feel each soaking-wet moment pass by like the heavy weight that pressed her heart. But before she had time to think, the growl's owner pounced! Jane screamed and fell backwards. As she struggled to get up, she observed that it was a huge jaguar. After jumping back up she watched in horror as the jaguar landed on Chris. Blinded by rage, she ran into the huge cat aided by Diana, and they pounded it with all their might, pushed on by Chris's screams. The awful growling and cries were too much. Jane fought with a helpless rage as tears blinded her vision.

Almost as quickly as it had started, it ended. The animal fell to the ground from the repeated blows to its head and Chris lay silent.

"Oh, God! Is he dead, Jane? I can't look."

Jane looked over at Chris's mutilated body and almost threw up. She began wiping her eyes off as tears continued to stain her face.

"Now we're never going to leave, ever!" Jane gasped. "Diana, look, he was reaching for that one gun of his. In fact, it's in his hand."

Diana started to moan and rolled over onto her side.

"I can't believe that Chris just got..." She was not able to finish her sentence. A fresh stream of tears started rolling down Jane's cheek. "He only fired one shot before; there must have been more left. Unless he was afraid of hitting one of us." A soft lump was growing in Jane's throat. She quickly put the gun down as she noticed Diana's condition.

"Oh, no. What's wrong, Diana?" Jane asked.

"I think I'm going to pass out." Diana had one hand over her eye.

"You can't die too!" Jane yelled hopelessly.

"Jane, look at my leg."

Jane moved closer to Diana and looked at the back of her left leg. It was hard to make out because of the darkness, but Jane could tell that Diana's leg had a series of long cuts running down it.

"Does it hurt a lot?" Jane asked; it was the only thing she could say.

"Not as much as my head, but what about you? Are you okay?"

Jane swallowed and nodded her head. All she had was a few marks and scratches.

"My eye, Jane," Diana said softly.

"Diana," Jane said, then whispered, "Diana, Diana."

Jane sat quietly, hoping Diana would wake up. Seeing that she was not responding, Jane picked her up and started limping away from the scene. After a half an hour of walking in the dark, surrounded by fear and sobbing softly to herself, she tripped over a tree root and fell to the ground. Falling hard, Jane collapsed and half unconscious went to sleep, hoping tomorrow would never come.

Leea stayed up all night racking her brain for an idea. She had no proof of anything and was very worried. If Jane was missing and Tom and Joe disappeared when she did, then where was she? Even though they claimed they didn't know anything, Leea wouldn't believe that for a second. They have to know something. Leea sat on her bed staring at the floor until an idea came to her.

Leea placed something into her pocket, then tiptoed down her hallway. Passing a few doors before she came to the guest bedroom, she slowly opened it. She heard the familiar squeak, and as she had predicted, there they were, awake.

"What are you doing here?" Tom said, slightly startled.

"The question is, what are you doing here?"

"Your mom invited us to stay," Joe said, uncertain.

"That's not what she meant, you idiot," Tom snapped.

"What then, huh?"

"I want to know what you did with Jane. I know about the picture and I want to know the truth," Leea said, fighting back her conscience's attempt in convincing her to flee.

"What did this Jane tell you?" Tom said slyly.

"She told me what I know and that's all I'm saying."

Tom sighed, seeing that this girl wasn't going to bend. "I guess it won't hurt if we tell; it's not going to change anything," Tom said, grinning. It seemed as though he was proud of himself and just wanted to gloat over how he had pulled off this scheme.

"What does that mean!" Leea said fearfully.

Tom took a deep breath. "We've been planning this for a long time. We had worked at this forever. We wanted to create something that no one would forget and something that we could walk away with. Were not saying that this crime will never be forgotten, but at least we'll be heroes. I mean, we convict the killer, get paid handsomely, plus the other money, and get famous. Everything was perfect, everything was almost done when..." Tom stopped and his eyes filled with disgust. "He got mad. He got mad at us for not sharing the money that the court was paying us because we were the lawyers. He claimed that none of this would have happened without him and that we wouldn't have gotten the job, but we weren't going to give him any."

"Yeah," Joe cut in, "we needed proof that it was him. So we had this picture taken about two weeks before the murder. I think Tom took it 'cause he wanted to see all the other occupants that were in the house. Anyway, we got it reprinted and changed the date to just a minute after the 911 call."

"Of course we got his finger prints on it," Tom added.

"Who's 'he' and how did you change the date?" Leea asked.

"Sam Norman."

"Who's Sam Norman?"

"He's the suspect; how come you didn't know that?" Tom said, surprised.

"I don't follow the case. All's I know is what Jane told me. Now, how did you change the date?"

"It was very simple," Joe said.

"But we aren't going to tell you."

"And why not?"

"'Cause we don't have to."

"What does this have to do with you kidnapping my friend?" Leea asked.

"Well, after that happened we were fine. Everything once again was great, now, I don't know how or why this happened, but the real picture was found." Tom shot a menacing sideways glance at Joe who turned and looked at the ground. "If I had the chance to find out how that happened I'd..." Tom stopped again and took a moment to vent his ever-increasing anger. "I mean, what an idiot not to destroy that picture! The next thing I know, these two girls are in front of the courthouse about to turn it in! I was not going to let these two ruin what we had worked so hard for; I took it, they grabbed it back and ran. We chased them and ended up at my jet. We put them on it and the guard that had chased us. Then we took off."

"Why, why would you do that?" Leea asked with a grin on her face that she couldn't hide.

"Everything was happening really fast and the guard was there, and the police were coming and there we were with the picture and two girls who knew too much," Joe said.

"But now I know; aren't you worried?"

"You don't have proof; you're just a girl upset about the murders," Joe answered.

"Murders?" Leea repeated, putting extra emphasis on the plural sound.

"Moving on," Tom interrupted. "We had been flying for a very long time; it was almost night. We had no idea what to do. Once we started running low on gas, we landed the plane in some desert in the middle of nowhere. We had gasoline for the plane in barrels, so we started to fill the plane up."

"Once we were almost done, one of those damn girls started the plane and took off!"

"And there we were, watching the plane fly away. In a different angle than the way we had come."

"Aren't you scared that they landed the plane and have already handed in the picture?" Leea said, puzzled.

"Nope," Tom replied, grinning.

Leea shuddered. "Why wouldn't you be?"

"Let's put it this way: we don't know why they haven't found the plane."

"I don't get it," Leea stated.

"Look, there was no way for them to land the plane. We jammed the steering wheel before we got out. It should have crashed by now, but I haven't heard anything."

"How could you do that? Jane must be fine!" Leea said as hot anger rose inside her.

"We didn't know that they were planning on taking off! We thought they were still tied up! It doesn't matter anyway; there's your answer and you can't do anything," Tom said as he settled back onto his bed.

"There is one thing that I don't think you two understand."

"Yeah, what's that?" Tom said carelessly.

"You don't even care about who the girls were."

"What's that matter?"

"Well, Jane was Myrtle McTerm's niece."

A silence followed as Tom and Joe tried to digest the information. Finally, Joe managed to get one word out, "What?"

"It's the truth, so now you guys know why it will be so important to help locate her, right? She's not just a missing girl; she's part of the case now." Leea stopped and added, "I'm sure everyone will think the criminals had something to do with it."

"That isn't true," Tom stuttered.

"How is that possible? Do we have to get hit by every stone?"

"Shut up, Joe," Tom said quietly.

"Just one more question."

"What? Make it quick, then leave; I don't have any more time for this."

"Did you guys murder Myrtle McTerm?"

"There was three of us and we were all in on it, but I'm not telling you anything else."

"Why not?"

"'Cause I don't have to."

Leea quietly exited the room. She closed the door slowly and began to walk to her room. She was very frightened; her heart was pounding and she could hear her breath as she tried to stop her eyes from filling with tears. She felt like running outside and far away from her house. Just thinking that there were two criminals, murderers, in her home was too much to bear.

She stopped cold in her hallway and began to think, "What if they change their minds and decide that they shouldn't have told me?" Her heart skipped a beat and frantically, she ran into her room and locked the door. She was more shaken than anything and was worried that she'd have to live with this secret. Pulling her blankets over herself, she laid her head on her pillow. Closing her eyes tight, Leea took a deep breath, hoping tomorrow would never come.

You don't have to accept the truth for it to be truth.

Chapter 20

Morning came. Bright rays of light slipped through the trees. Small clouds stood still on the light blue sky. Loud chirping was issued from a nearby tree as blue birds soared across it. The still air was overlooked as the sunny dawn lit the neighboring lawns.

Heather sat upright on her bed listening to the noises of nature through her window. She glanced at her clock; it read 10:46 a.m. Yawning, she stood up and left her room. As she walked down the stairs, Heather could hear her mom talking on the phone. Heather stopped and listened.

"That is something, isn't it? I don't know what to say...yes, that really doesn't make sense. I hope they do! All right, bye then." Once Heather's mom had hung up the phone, Heather came into view.

"Who were you talking to?"

"Mrs. McTerm. She said that Barry Lonad called her and..."

"They found Jane!?" Heather's heart skipped a beat.

"No, they found Tom Hankar and Joe Tremmer, two of the five missing."

"If they all disappeared together, how come they only found them?" Heather said, considerably downhearted.

"That's what we don't understand. Mrs. McTerm and I are hoping that they will get some answers out of those two men."

"I hope they do," Heather said glumly.

Heather sat down at her kitchen table and began to pour cereal into a bowl. She looked up and asked her mom, "Where could they be?"

"Where could who be, dear?

"Jane and Diana."

"Honey, I don't know. It makes absolutely no sense to me that they could find two people and not the others. I guess it could happen, but then Tom and Joe must know where Jane and Diana are or at least have some idea. What I just don't get is if Jane and Diana are by themselves, why couldn't they call or something?"

"I'm not hungry," Heather said as she pushed away her cereal. Standing up, she slid in her chair.

"Why not? You haven't eaten anything yet."

"I think that if I take a nap I'll feel better." Heather didn't know why she had said that. She hated sleeping. It was her worst fear, and yet, she knew that it was the only thing she could do. She needed answers. Lying back down in her bed, Heather closed her eyes. She dosed off after about ten minutes.

Black was everywhere. All there was was the thick-clouded black. No voice, no blurred colors. Then the rose appeared. Lying there in all its beauty, as blinding white as it was before. It hadn't withered at all. Heather stared at the rose, puzzled. The more she stared at it, the prettier it became, the fresher it looked. Nothing else could be seen.

"What is this!" Heather yelled into the darkness. She didn't understand why all there was was the rose and the black that surrounded it. She tried to think and ponder as to why.

"I don't understand. Why is just this rose, your present, the only thing I see! Where are Jane and Diana, can't you tell me!" Still no answer. She tried one more time. "So, I guess you're gone. Not enough imagination left for you! And what is this rose still doing here! I don't want it!" Heather ran up to the rose with all her might and tried to stomp on it. But, right before she could, something threw her backwards. She didn't see what it was, but she knew what it had to be.

"You fool! This rose isn't for you! It's a present, I already told you that! I wasn't planning on not talking to you ever again. The damage has been done, I am done, and you caused it all, so remember that!"

"I don't believe you! I refuse to believe that this is real!"

"You don't believe? Well, when you find out just how nicely your friends fared, maybe then you'll believe me! You don't have to accept the truth for it to be truth!"

"What did you do to them? You try to blame me but it's you! You're just too weak to face it!" Heather screamed.

"No, the question is, what did *you* do to them! It was your mind, your imagination! And I already told you what you must pay for being so slow! For not understanding the poem, for not caring enough to save your friend's life!"

"But I do..."

"Don't talk to me anymore! You did what you did, and now I have given my present and will be silent! But remember, every time you close your eyes I am there! Maybe I'll visit someone else just so you know that this isn't over yet! Every time you blink I am watching you! I never leave a soul once I am in it! You can never escape me!" the voice screamed harshly.

After Heather had been thrown, spots started to appear in front of her. She had hit the wall of blackness even though she never realized that there was one. Her heart was beating twice as fast. Everything became dark, and even the rose disappeared.

Beep. Beep. Beep. Beep. Beep.

Heather opened her eyes and took stock of her surroundings. To her left was a heart monitor that kept beating at a steady pace. Just beyond the monitor was a window with white curtains. As she looked to her right, she realized where she was.

"Are you feeling dizzy?" a nurse with dirty blonde hair asked her.

"Not really. Why am I here?"

"You tell me," the nurse replied, looking straight at Heather.

149

"Why would I know?"

"Why? Dear, people don't just sit and get a concussion."

Heather looked strangely at the nurse. "I last thing I remember is falling asleep." Heather caught her breath remembering how the voice had thrown her. "That was just a dream."

"What? Well, when you were falling asleep you were probably losing consciousness and just thinking that. So, what were you doing before you started falling asleep?"

"I was walking upstairs to my room."

"That's got to be it. You must have forgotten; it happens a lot. You were walking upstairs and tripped."

"No, that can't be it because I remember being in bed." But Heather's words fell on deaf ears as the nurse exited the room.

Heather closed her eyes, then snapped them open as she remembered what the voice had said. She took a deep breath as she confirmed that her dreams had to be true. They had to be utterly and completely true. Heather shuddered. "But how could a dream hurt me? I don't understand. How could it have thrown me and made me end up in a hospital?" Heather whispered to herself.

"Honey, you're all right! That was a hard fall you took!" Heather's mom said as she entered the room accompanied by the same nurse that Heather had just met.

"But Mom..."

"Oh, Heather, I feel so sorry! First your ankle, now this!"

Heather felt a chill as the words echoed around her: "First your ankle..."

"You must be cold," The nurse said, seeing Heather shudder. "The doctor still isn't sure if she'll stay the night or not."

"Could we have some time alone please?" Heather's mom asked. The nurse nodded, then left.

"Mom, you've got to believe me on this one. The nurse isn't right. I didn't fall, I'm sure of it. You have to..."

"I do."

"You believe that I didn't fall?" Heather said slowly.

"Well, who do you think found you laying in bed?"

"How did you know I wasn't sleeping?"

"I tried to wake you up. Now, what could have happened was that something was wrong inside your head that caused you to pass out. That's what I want to believe, but that still..." Her mom stopped and took a deep breath. "But that still doesn't explain that lump on your head. Heather, how did this happen?"

"I was dreaming, and in my dream, the voice was yelling at me."

"What are you talking about?"

"Mom, you found me laying in bed, unconscious, now listen. I was having another dream, a dream that was more real than the one before it. I was alone in dark blackness, and the voice got mad and threw me. I hit some kind of wall and started seeing bright colors. I kept talking to the voice even though I could barely think, and then I woke up here. I know that it was my dream's fault, but I don't quite get it."

"I don't know if I believe that, but for the moment, I don't have any other ideas that make more sense."

"I know that that's what happened."

"Well, why don't you just lay here and rest. I'm going to make some phone calls and then I'll be back."

"Okay, bye." Heather settled back and looked at the ceiling. She averted her eyes and began to watch the window, looking outside at the swaying trees and the cars that drove along the road. Yawning, she blinked, and like a bolt of lightning, the white rose flashed before her. Her eyes opened wide and she tried to close them again, but she saw nothing. She tried many more times, but all she saw was a barren blank.

Some may think that there is a calming after the storm, a blue sky that appears and washes away the darkness. But, there is always a shrouded mist with a tint of forever unchanging gray.

Chapter 21

Pushed by curiosity, a small monkey flew from tree to tree, getting closer and closer to a nearby tent. It was placed on a wide path that had been beaten down by travelers and animals alike. One tent flap had been pulled up and hung over a nearby branch. The monkey dropped from the tree it had been hanging from and landed to the right of the tent. It sat intently waiting for a noise or some movement. A high-pitched scream that startled the monkey was issued from the tent, and it turned and fled.

"Sshhhh. It's okay. Just count to ten."

"Oh, God! One, two, three, four... make it stop hurting!"

"Is that better?"

"Yes, that hurt! That hurt a lot!"

"Just lay there, don't move."

"You sound different...wait, who are you?"

"My name's Becky Lind. I don't want you to talk much so just give me a first name."

"Diana."

"Diana, I explore various parts of the rainforest for a living. I had just started out on another expedition and I stumbled over you and that girl."

"Jane! How is she?"

"She's not as hurt as you. Now, I called back and a helicopter should be here to take you two to a hospital."

Diana froze. Her eyes had a forlorn look, and as she stared at the ceiling of the tent the realization of what was going on came to her. She began to whisper excitedly, "We're getting out of here! Oh, I can't believe it! We're leaving, oh, God! Hey, Jane did you hear that?" Tears began to slide down Diana's cheek.

"She can't hear you; she's still unconscious. Stop talking; you're only making things worse. Don't answer this, but I would like an explanation on how you two got here."

Diana wanted to answer her but felt very weak. She had a patch over one eye and bandages over most of her legs, arms and back.

Diana was overcome with emotion. She lay on a blanket trying not to move, but the task seemed impossible. All she could think about was that she, *she* was going home. She could see her friends again and her family. She wasn't going to die; she was going home. She had felt so ill from being surrounded by muggy air and having no one around but Jane and Chris. Also constantly wondering if her next move would be her last. Nothing was real, everything was too much, and now she was going home. Her mind went back to Chris, but she had to vanquish him from her mind. It was all too hard.

Jane moaned and slowly opened her eyes. Becky had placed a wet cloth over her forehead. After Jane opened her eyes, she realized that she was in a tent. Without moving her head, she spoke slowly, "Diana, where are we?"

"You are in good hands," Becky replied.

Jane tried to sit up and see who had said that, but quickly regretted it as a sharp pain flooded through her head.

"Jane, it's Diana. We're leaving! This lady found us, we're going home!"

"My name's Becky Lind," the lady confirmed politely.

"We're, we're, going home? We're leaving!" Jane said hopefully but still not fully awake.

"Yes, you will be brought to a hospital once a helicopter gets here," Becky said.

"How can a helicopter get here?" Diana asked.

"I told you not to talk," Becky said, but this time much more commanding.

"Why can't she talk?" Jane asked.

"It's just better for her to rest. I'll answer her question though. The helicopter is going to land farther away in a clearing and then a squad will come in and get you."

Jane couldn't believe what she was hearing. She felt as though it was a dream, some kind of cruel trick that her mind was playing on her. She tried to breathe the air and hear the sounds to confirm that this was reality. Her head throbbed, and she winced as a fresh flow of pain hit her. Not being able to focus and still confused, she tried to look at Diana. She hadn't seen Diana's face in the light after the incident. When Jane moved her head to look at Diana, she was glad that she couldn't focus. It was a horrid sight. Becky had patched it up as best she could, but you could still see the flesh that had been torn away from her face and arms. Blood stained her all over, and as Jane went to look away, she saw why Becky did not want her to talk. To the left of Diana's stomach a sharp branch about eight inches long had been forced through her. Jane felt nauseated.

Then she drew in a sharp breath. "That's my fault. I fell. I was so tired that I just collapsed. You must have fallen on it. Oh, I'm sorry," Jane whispered. Diana didn't hear her, but Becky did. Still not sure on what had happened to Jane and Diana, Becky felt sorry for her and began to talk softly.

"It's not your fault, don't ever think that. And don't worry, she can't feel the pain. I gave her medicine that I keep with me. She is losing a lot of blood though. I'm doing my best."

"You mean she's going to die," Jane whispered as tears began to surface in her eyes.

"Let's just say that the sooner the helicopter gets here, the better. Now, I still don't know what could have happened to you to make you pass out from exhaustion. What kind of an expedition were you on?"

"I did?" Jane said dizzily.

"What? Oh, well, yes, you did. Now lie back down before you pass out again."

Jane obliged.

The helicopter couldn't be heard through the trees, but a few minutes later, six men came running up to the tent. They immediately put each girl on a stretcher and headed her back down the path. Becky followed because the men insisted that she answer a series of questions. It took some time before they came to the clearing and loaded everyone onto the helicopter.

Jane painfully lifted her head and took a look at the surrounding vegetation. As she took one last look, all that she saw was green, faint colors and sounds too far off to understand. The trees were as high as ever, and the hum was still there. But it didn't give Jane the same helpless feeling that she had felt before. It gave her a feeling of relief. She still couldn't see right, and the colors started to blur together. She saw the forest as a giant blur of dark greens, all swirled together in an unrealistic manner. Jane put her head back down and closed her eyes.

Leea had sat quietly during breakfast. She hadn't said a word as she helped her mom clean up. She had a depressed and worried look on her face. Her mom stared at her oddly.

"Leea, why you acting so strange?"

"No reason."

"Yes, there's a reason. I know you. Is it about Jane? You must feel badly about her, but don't worry, I'm sure she'll be fine."

At that moment Tom and Joe entered the kitchen. Leea stared at them with hurtful eyes. They took the liberty to sit at the kitchen table and help themselves to cereal and milk.

"You two help yourselves, and then I'll drive you up to the airport."

"Thank you, Rachell, you've been so kind. You have a wonderful daughter."

Leea glared at them and said, "Mom, can I talk to you in the family room?"

"Sure," Rachell answered as they left the room.

"Mom, I think I have to go down to New York with those two."

"Why?"

"It's very important, Mom."

"I don't know what to say."

"Remember how you use to tell me never to lie because every lie holds a lie that can't be proven?"

"Yes," her mom replied slowly.

"Well, I know something very important. It will fix a mixed-up lie. It could even help Jane."

"I don't know what to tell you. I can't fly you down there. It would cost a fortune."

"I know, I know."

They reentered the kitchen and found Tom and Joe washing their dishes in the sink.

"Why, thank you! That was very polite of you two. We should be leaving now; Leea, would you like to come?" Rachell asked.

"Yes."

Leea had answered too fast, Tom thought to himself.

The airport was a good twenty miles away. It seemed like an eternity to Tom and Joe as they felt the tension between them and Leea. As Rachell drove, she tried to make small talk with the two of them. They tried to answer with politeness and a smile, but Leea could tell that her mom was driving them crazy. Finally, they arrived at the airport. After parking, Tom and Joe jumped out of the car and started briskly walking away.

"Wait!" Rachell yelled.

First they paused, then turned back around.

"Did ya honestly think that I'd just leave you two at an airport that you've never been to before?"

Tom looked at the ground and mumbled, "Of course not."

Once they walked in, a huge crowd surrounded them. Barry Lonad appeared and was about to take them away to their plane when Leea pulled on his sleeve.

"Yes?" Barry said.

"I think I know something important about the case."

"How important?"

"Very important."

"I don't have time for this now. If it's that important, then you'll have to call someone and report it."

"You have to listen to me, please!"

"I can't, I'm sorry." It was hard to hear above the melee of people and cameras. Leea could tell that Barry wanted to be on his way but didn't want to ignore her.

"Mom, I have to fly down there, they have to know the truth."

"What truth?" Rachell said.

"Mom, Jane told me something very important that I didn't believe until now. I have to go," Leea yelled so her mom could hear.

"You know I don't have enough money."

"Mom, please." Leea looked desperate, and her mom could see it.

"I don't know how it could be this important, but as I see that it is, I might as well let you go. I was saving up so you could go back and visit your friends for your birthday anyway."

Leea walked up to a travel agent and asked when the next flight was leaving. As she talked Barry Lonad walked by and saw her.

"What are you doing?"

"I was trying to get a flight to New York, but they don't have any seats left on the next flight."

"It's that important?"

"I also know the McTerm family very well."

"I suppose you could come on our plane. We have extra seats, but you'd have to pay your own way."

Leea looked dumbfounded at Barry. "Really?"

"Well, if you need to get to New York this bad, then I don't mind. You can tell me your story once we get there. I don't have time now."

"Thank you so much!"

Barry then turned to face Rachell. "Thank you for keeping Tom and Joe at your house."

"I should be thanking you for letting my daughter go with you."

Barry stopped for a moment and replied, "That's your daughter?"

"Well, yes."

"I see. I didn't know that. For being so kind and compliant, I'll let her come for free."

Leea couldn't believe what was happening. As she walked through the airport, being trailed by hundreds of people, she knew that this was definitely the best possible thing that could have happened today. Once they were boarded, Joe finally realized that Leea was still with them.

"Tom, she's on the plane!"

"What!?" Tom turned around to find Leea sitting one row behind them.

"Barry, this girl sneaked onto our plane."

"No, she didn't. I'm letting her come because I want to question her and..."

"Can't you do that over the phone!"

"Calm down, Tom, what's wrong with you?"

"Just a little shook up, I guess."

"Well, I would have done that, but you saw the crowd, and that was with me trying to keep it a secret, I had to think fast. Plus, her mom has been so kind and she said that she had something important to tell me. I didn't want to just leave."

Tom's mouth almost dropped open. "Since when do you do stuff like this, huh?"

Barry looked at him oddly. "Tom, I don't see what the big deal is; she could really help the case."

It took all Tom's strength to keep quiet. Joe looked worried and didn't know what to do.

"I'm surprised you guys are so mad. You remember what you did when you had to think fast, don't you?" Leea whispered to Tom and Joe.

"What are you going to tell?" Tom said, his face tight. "You can't prove anything. The reason we told you is because it's all so crazy. It has so many holes. No one will buy it as truth."

"It's not what I'm going to tell, it's what I'm going to do."

"Which would be what?" Tom glared at her, baffled.

"I'm not telling."

"Why?"

"'Cause I don't have to." Satisfied, Leea sat back in her seat, gave a mischievous smile and felt a ball of butterflies circle in her stomach.

"I'm gonna shoot her, I'm gonna shoot her now. I can't take this!" Tom whispered harshly to Joe.

"Try to relax."

Tom gave Joe a look that could've killed him.

The flight was long, and all the while Leea tried to think about what she was going to say. Trying to forget her worries, she leaned over and gazed out her window. She remembered the last time she was on a plane. When she turned nine in the cold month of November, her grandmother passed away. She never knew her dad or his family, so when her mom's mother died it was incredibly hard. This was the only time that she could remember her mom spending that much money at once. They flew down to Florida and went to the funeral. She remembered her mom wishing that they could've driven, but it would have taken too long.

Leea studied the outside clouds as they glided softly over them. It looked as though they were soaring over mountains and valleys that had been painted a barren white. The clouds swirled in all directions and spread over everything. They resembled rolling hills, and the sun made them shine and look even more surreal. "I hope that everyone will be able to see the other side of a cloud in their life," Leea said to herself, then slowly nodded off as she waited for the plane to reach its long-awaited destination.

The light at the end of the tunnel may turn out to be bittersweet.

Chapter 22

"Well, she has various bruised bones and a broken leg, the other one, ah, didn't, didn't, make it, we tried everything and..."

"Doctor."

"Yes?"

"I see that you're busy, but we need you in room 207 for a moment."

"Alright," the doctor replied, then turned back toward the man that he'd been talking to and said softly, "I'm sorry about your son and daughter; I will be back in a minute."

The doctor was African American and his nametag read Doctor Harald Walters, 26 years of experience.

As he entered room 207, four other doctors and the nurse that had gone to notify him confronted him. The room was full of x-rays and papers. It was dimly lit so the x-rays would show clearly on the yellowed screen. There was a table in the center of the room that the doctors had surrounded. One doctor looked up from some documents he'd been reading just long enough to say in a low and concerned voice, "Doctor Walters, we would like your input on this. We have found ourselves in a very vague situation. A researcher was recently sent on an expedition into the Amazon and had to return after one night. She did not help us too much when we tried to question her.

We are not one to be surprised; I mean, we have seen everything, including this type of injury. What we can't figure out is who we are treating or how they ending up where they did. No one from any recent expedition has been able to identify them, and we are all very puzzled."

"I'm not quite following."

"Look at these x-rays," the doctor said, pointing to four x-rays. The x-rays were of a badly bruised stomach. The ribs seemed to be slightly cracked. The doctor waited a few minutes before speaking again. "What do you think happened to this person, Doctor Walters?"

"Well, it could be a number of things. Abuse maybe."

"No, it's not from abuse, and I can almost assure you that it's not the number of things that you were thinking of. The girl that I took these x-rays from was basically in shock. She was unable to assist me with any personal information or any useful information for that matter. She gave me a very uneasy feeling and I would like to get to the bottom of this."

"You're saying two girls? What age?"

"We estimated them to be fifteen to eighteen and the one that I talked to is, when compared to the other, doing excellent."

"What condition is the other one in?"

"She's in the emergency room, and there's no guarantee that she'll live."

"That's very sad news; you know, I just had a death of a twelve-year-old boy. Doctor, I think that if you want to get over the mystery of where these two came from, what happened to them and so on, the best thing to do would be to let me visit one. Is the one in better condition stable?"

"Yes, she can be visited. We are still keeping a close eye on her, though. Follow me, Doctor Walters, I will show you to her room."

Once the other doctor reached the room, he turned and left, leaving Doctor Walters to enter when he pleased. Doctor Walters turned the doorknob and walked inside.

The room was white. It was as white as a barren field carpeted with snow. There were white walls and ceilings, white curtains and sheets. The only thing that gave way to color was a painting that hung in the center of one wall. The painting had a vast ocean painted on it with tiny sail boats floating near the shore. The painting was done with a bird's eye view, and in the middle of the ocean, a green tail lay protruding out of the water, unknown to the occupants on the boats.

A weak and slightly audible voice came from the bed in the center of the room. "Who is it?"

"My name is Doctor Herald Walters. You can call me Herald."

"How's Diana?"

"Diana?"

"Yes, my friend. She's here, right?"

"Oh, you must mean the other girl. She's doing, ah, fairly well."

"She has to be fine, she has to," she said in a weak whisper.

"What's your name?"

"Jane McTerm." Jane's first clear thought in days hit her. "My family, my home."

"Jane, I would like to ask you some questions. Is that okay?"

"Yeah, I guess. That is so annoying!" Jane shirked as she pointed to her heartbeat monitor.

Doctor Walters took a few steps forward so he could view the girl. She was more bandaged up than he had expected and looked very out of breath.

He pulled a chair over and sat down. "Try not to let it bother you," he said, looking at the monitor. "Where do you live?"

"New Jersey."

"Where?"

"USA."

"I would have thought you'd live here."

"Yes, that's what everyone thinks."

"Why are you here then?"

"I don't know; it makes no sense."

"Why did you decide to come here?"

"Decide?" Jane's lips parted slowly. "Hardly."

"I don't know how to go about this. You're not giving me any answers."

"You're not asking the right questions."

"All right, how's this: how did you end up in this hospital?"

Jane's face faded as panic began to creep up on her.

"What?" Doctor Walters asked.

"Where's my jacket?"

"I don't know."

"You have to find it! There is something so valuable in one of the pockets!"

"I'll try to find out, you just stay calm and breathe steadily. Don't work yourself up." The doctor hurriedly stood up and left the room.

Jane lay in the bed with her hospital gown on, trying fervently to stay calm. She closed her eyes and wished for a moment of silence, a moment to look around and confirm that all was not lost. Without the picture, their entire escapade would be in vain.

The emergency room doctor breathed in a sigh of relief. It had been eight long hours since the patient had first arrived, and finally they had finished their first operation successfully.

"It looks like that went well," a nurse said to the doctor that had performed the operation. "I suppose, but look at her, and we don't even know her name."

"Or where she came from. I'm telling you, this is the oddest thing I've seen, ever."

"I just hope she makes it."

"Long time before we'll be able to determined that."

"I know."

Diana lay there, unconscious and not able to breathe on her own yet. A patch had been placed over her eye and a thick bandage over her leg.

Becky Lind stood outside of the emergency room waiting for the results. She had decided to stay because she was so curious about the girls. She looked up as the doctor exited the emergency room.

"How is she doing?"

"She's still with us, but we have to keep her in intensive care."

"Do you know what happened to her?"

"I think she was attacked by something, and that would explain the deep cuts, but I'm not sure about how that object got lodged in her side."

"You mean that piece of branch?"

"Yes."

"I'm pretty sure she tripped, because when the other one woke up, she said something about tripping and it being her fault. I just wish I knew the whole story."

"We will find out soon enough."

"I hope so."

"I have a favor to ask you, Miss...?"

"Becky Lind, you can call me Becky."

"Becky, you know the girls better than any of us."

"I don't know them at all."

"You still know them better because at least they know your name, and I think they'll be able to communicate with you better."

"What do you want me to do?"

"I want you to go onto the third floor and visit the other one, try to find the phone number so we can call the parents. I would also like for you to try and figure out why they ended up where they did."

"I'll try. What's the room number?"

"I'm not sure. You'll have to ask that nurse over there," he said, pointing down the hall.

Becky followed the nurse into the elevator and through the hallways until they reached Jane's room. Becky placed her hand on the doorknob, took a deep breath and entered.

"Who is it?"

"Becky Lind; do you remember me?"

"Of course, you saved my life."

Becky stood silent for a moment, not sure how to respond. "I'm glad you remember me." She stammered, "Before we can contact your family, I need to know a few things."

"Like what?" Jane said softly while staring at the ceiling.

Becky looked at the ground, not knowing where to start. Jane looked sideways at her and then began to voice her story. "My aunt was murdered, and I found a valuable piece of evidence."

"Oh, I'm sorry to hear that." After a moment's pause Becky asked, "What was it?"

"A picture. I was watching the trial on TV and I saw the same exact picture on the trial as evidence. I can still feel that odd feeling in the tips of my fingers. My picture had a different date proving that the people who turned it in had tampered with it to frame someone. Later on, when I realized that this picture could clear the man being convicted, I decided to bring it to the courthouse, but, but..."

Becky just waited.

"The criminals got to us first."

"What?" Becky said, quite puzzled about where this story was going.

"But they got to us first. The criminals. They chased us. A policeman had followed us and he was calling for back up, I think, so they put us on a jet and took off."

"Just like that? Isn't it a little harder to take off like that?"

"It all happened too fast. All I remember is being in the air and the time going by minute by minute, second by second, hour by hour. Then they landed it to refuel. I went to the front, and I was covered with fear." Jane shuddered. "I can still feel the pounding my heart made, like a hollow drum, but I got the thing started and took off. I was going to try and turn it around, but when I put my hands on the steering wheel, they came in contact with cold steel. I looked down and they had put a bar across it so it couldn't be turned. All we could do was go straight. There was no way to get it off. I could pull the steering wheel a little, but that only made it go higher."

"But how did you end up here?"

"The plane ran out of gas..." It looked like Jane was going to say more, but she stopped and started staring at the ceiling.

"You crashed into the rainforest?"

"We parachuted out before the plane crashed."

Becky could tell that Jane didn't want to push the issue any further, but she tried one more question. "So, it was just you and the other girl?"

Jane's eyes welled up and she took a gasp of air. Turning her head toward Becky, she just shook her head.

Becky's heart sank as she saw Jane's head shake. She was overcome with curiosity but tired to hide it. She had just enough information now and only needed Jane's identification.

"Jane, I know that you must want to go home or talk with your family, so I need your phone number. I also would like your address and the names of your parents."

Jane began to slowly release the information. She gave Becky her phone number as a small feeling of joy crept inside her that covered the trauma of her recent escapade.

Diana lay on the bed in the emergency room while the monitors around her kept beeping and clicking as the time wore on, except one. It began to slow, and Diana's breath became more ragged. Beep, beep, beep.. beep... beep.... beep.............

The chain that falls behind in an endless trail of textures and moments shall forever beckon to its owner. There is no way to remove such a chain, and it is up to the wearer to decide if it shall be cast of iron or velvet. Though the owner may never know at which point he chose which fate to bear.

Chapter 23

A high whistling noise pierced the silent air, cutting through everything like a steel whistle that whipped through the clouded atmosphere. She fell to the ground with thick, unwilling blood pouring steadily from her neck. The clouds from high above let small droplets of rain fall onto her limp body. Her sweet smile disappeared and her eyes misted over with a faint gray. She lay on the cold cement sidewalk with no more words left inside her and her eyes with their new dull appearance finally closing. Silence took over once again, a chilling, heart-stopping, dead silence that was broken by Mrs. McTerm's cry.

Mrs. McTerm awoke with a start. She had sweat beading down her face. Visibly shaken, she put on her slippers and light blue bathrobe. Standing up, she began to walk down the hallways making her way toward the kitchen. Once she entered the kitchen, she looked at the microwave. Its digital clock read 4:39 a.m. She was seldom in the kitchen at this hour. Feeling her way toward the light switch, she flicked it on. Walking over to her counter, she put two pieces of bread into the toaster. Turning, she looked at the window that had been placed in the side of the kitchen. It was stained glass, and in the sunny mornings it glowed radiantly. The colors were bright reds, yellows, blues and greens. They were in tiny specks all over the window to create a blended look where the beginning and end seemed impossible to find.

Pop! Mrs. McTerm nearly jumped out of her skin. The toast had sprung out of the toaster, black and dark brown. Mumbling to herself, she put both pieces into the garbage and turned the toaster's dial down. She took one last glance at the stained glass window; everything started to blend slightly and mix in an unreal way. Trying to shake it off, Mrs. McTerm exited the kitchen and began to make her way back through the halls. Searching for Mark's room, she started to feel lost. Soon Mrs. McTerm began to get frustrated; she couldn't find his room or her own. Puzzled because she thought she knew every hallway, she began to slow down. In the stark darkness, Mrs. McTerm walked with one hand gliding across the wall, feeling for a light switch. A cool breeze blew past her, and for a moment it felt refreshing. Crunch, crunch. Mrs. McTerm looked down and her face turned a pale white. To her horror, there, lying in front of her, were broken pieces of glass. She looked up at the now shattered window. Drawing in a sharp breath, she heard something go crunch behind her. Turning slowly, she saw a dark shape moving toward her from the end of the hall. It took fast, short steps and then stopped, the blackness hardly outlining its unidentifiable shape. A freezing wind blew passed Mrs. McTerm, and suddenly the shape began to move again, this time with slow, pounding steps, a shining object dangling from one side of it. Right as it stepped into the pale moonlight...

Mrs. McTerm sat bolt upright, breathing in ragged breaths. She found herself sitting in bed with sunlight pouring through the windows. Trying to erase the horrifying feeling that lurked inside her, she found it to be impossible.

"Just a dream, just a dream. Clam down, calm down."

"Honey?" Jake said uncertainly.

"Jake, it was awful. I dreamt that someone was shot and I thought I was awake, but I wasn't and then this guy, he broke in and he had a knife or something and then I woke up. It was so scary, just awful," she said as small sobs escaped her breath.

"It's alright. It was just a dream."

"That was what was so scary. At first I knew I was dreaming, well, I didn't know but, I, well..."

"What you're trying to say is?"

"You know when you're having a dream, I mean it still seems real, but it isn't reality and you can tell. Here's the strange part: when I was having my first dream I knew I was having a nightmare, but when I dreamt that someone had broken in, I had gone into the kitchen to make toast first. When the toast popped up, I could smell that it had been burnt, and when I stepped on the glass, I felt the breeze on my neck. I just don't understand it."

"I'm sure you just got scared. It's just been so hard with Jane and Diana missing. I can hardly stand it each day. It's like I'm dying all over again. I can't help but think that we could've prevented this, maybe we could've not let them go, maybe then they would still be here."

"Don't say that, Jake. It's hard enough without you reminding me that they could be here right now if we had just said no." Looking out the window, her face, now stained with tears, didn't brighten in the slightest when she saw the beautiful spring morning. The fluffy clouds, the birds' soft song, the endless rolling hills far off in the distance, all the beauty in the world lay wasted on Mrs. McTerm's eyes.

"I want my old life back. Right when I had everything, I lost it. When I finally thought that life was going to be great, that everything was finally perfect, everything crumbled. If we hadn't come into any money, if we hadn't bought this house, if the moving van hadn't dropped anything, if they had told Jane to send the picture, if..."

"The crime had never taken place," Jake said, staring at Mrs. McTerm.

"It's hard to say where this all began. I'm just really shaken from that dream. It was so strange, so bizarre, so real."

Heather's Mom had been driving for some time. It was a long drive from the hospital to their house. Heather sat in the backseat silently. She had been released from the hospital the next day. The bandage on her head covered most of her right eye. She had a constant headache, which beat her skull with an even pace. She looked out the window, trying to enjoy the outside scenery. It was one of the most glorious days. The sun shone radiantly on the treetops, making them glisten below the cloudless sky. Warm air flew past the swaying grass. Heather rolled down her window, trying to breath in the fresh air. The freshness in the breeze reminded Heather of summer. The heat from the sun traveled through her, and the crisp air ruffled the trees as they swayed from side to side.

"Heather, the doctor said that you should rest."

"What does that doctor know? Nothing."

"Heather, anyone could tell that you need rest."

"Mom, does a white rose serve any specific purpose?"

"A white rose?"

"Yeah."

"Well, it can be use for hundreds of different things. I don't know of anything where you would be requested to bring a white rose, if that's what you mean."

"Do you think we could stop at the McTerms' and see how they're doing?"

"If you want to, but only for a little. I want to get you home."

"Thanks."

As they drove toward the McTerms', Heather began to feel something welling inside her. Her eyes began to turn red, and for the umpteenth time she felt a weight being dropped on her throat. She tried not to cry about Jane. She tried to think that Jane would be home safe and sound, but as the days rolled on, she began to think more on the memories than anything else.

"It's so good of you to come!" Mrs. McTerm said as she greeted them at the door.

"Heather and I were driving home from the hospital and..."

"Why were you at the hospital? Oh my goodness! What happened to your head, Heather?"

"I was thrown and hit a wall."

"We can discuss it later," Heather's mom said, unsure of how she would explain it.

"Can you come in?" Mrs. McTerm asked.

"For a little, if you don't mind."

They sat in a small but comfortable room. It was one that the McTerms rarely went in. It had light brown walls and a creamy carpet. There was a small fireplace on the opposite wall from the door. A table with wooden legs and a glass top, two couches and an older looking lamp that sat on a small oak table all stood silently.

Not quite sure on how to start the conversation, Heather finally spoke up, "Mrs. McTerm, I miss Jane so much. I wanted to come over to talk to you and ask you if there is a word on where she might be."

"The only thing I can tell you is what you already know. They found two of the five missing. I called and tried to tell the police why Jane had gone down there in the first place. I said how they were convinced that the two were criminals and that they had proof, but it was a lost cause. No one would believe anything. I guess I didn't really expect them to."

Seeing that Mrs. McTerm wasn't going to tell her anything new, she decided to try something different. "Have you had any dreams lately?"

"Heather," her mom said disapprovingly.

"I did have one last night that was odd. It seemed so real and so scary."

"What happened in it?"

"Well, the first part of it was..." Mrs. McTerm stopped, her eyes turned red, and she breathed in short choppy breaths.

"Sorry, I didn't know it would upset you," Heather said, feeling rather guilty.

"No, it's alright. I'll just skip that part, that wasn't what felt so strange anyway. It was my next dream." Taking a deep breath, she began again, "I thought that I had just woken up and I went downstairs to the kitchen. After I had tried to make myself some toast, I walked back upstairs. I couldn't find my room or anyone else's. It was the weirdest thing. Then I stepped on something. I looked down and saw that it was glass. I had slippers on, so I didn't cut myself. Anyway, as I looked up, I felt a draft on my face, and that's when I realized that the window had been broken. I can still feel the icy fear that swept over me as I heard someone's footsteps behind me. I turned around and there was this thing standing behind me. The dark figure raised its hand, in it was a knife or something, and then I woke up."

"I don't see what this has to do with anything," Heather's mom voiced.

"I'm glad I got to tell someone. When I told Jake, he just laughed."

"Maybe we should be going."

"Heather does need to get some rest," Mrs. McTerm replied as she showed them to the door.

"Bye, Mrs. McTerm."

"Bye, hope you feel better soon. Come back whenever you like. I could use the company."

Once they were home, Heather ran to her room none too quickly. Her throbbing head wouldn't allow her to make any sudden movements. As she entered her room, she closed the door behind her. Sitting on her bed, Heather began talking to the silence.

"Look, I need you to answer my question. You must. I can't let you start doing this to her. You just can't. You have to talk to me. Have you entered her mind? Oh, what am I saying? Have I lost my mind? Am I going insane? I can't believe that I think some evil being has taken over my imagination! But what else makes sense? It all felt so real. I don't care if you're not real. I have to believe because if I don't then I'm probably wrong. Does that even make sense? I know that you said you weren't ever coming back, and I really don't want you to, but I need to talk to you." Heather stopped. She listened to the silence. It never answered.

The silence cut through everything. Heather could feel it as it took over. It was stronger than visible things and was immortal. Nothing could erase silence, just cover it. But coverings faded away and one was always left with what was once buried. Silence could not be demolished. It would always follow, hidden beneath the voices, the commotion, the speeches, and the laughter.

"Heather! Heather!"

Heather raced downstairs to find her mom on the phone, tears sliding down her cheek. As Heather looked closer, she saw the smile that played on her mom's face.

"What is it? Are you happy or sad?"

"Happy? I'm overjoyed! The McTerms just got a phone call; they found Jane and Diana."

The shock sent wild chills coursing through Heather's body. Her mind was thrown into a blur. Everything those dreams had told her about losing a friend. About killing those around her for being careless. The voice that she had believed in, the nightmares she couldn't explain. All false?

"Mom, you're sure?"

"Yes, honey, yes!"

"Can we see them?"

"Hold on, I'll ask."

"When can we see them, and where have they been? Oh, really...but how...are you quite sure...okay. Yes, we'll be there. Bye, then."

"What's wrong?"

"Jane and Diana were found in the, the Amazon rainforest, in ah, South America." She said it slowly as if afraid of looking stupid.

"Are you sure you heard right?"

"Positive. They got a long-distance call from a doctor who said that they had both girls in a local hospital."

"How did they end up there?"

"Apparently, no one knows. The police are going to look into it because they believe that this is linked to the other disappearances."

Heather just nodded. She knew that her mom was talking about Tom Hankar and Joe Tremmer.

"Mrs. McTerm is trying to find out when Jane and Diana can be returned home."

"What kind of condition are they in?"

"Well, I hadn't thought of that. Mrs. McTerm didn't say. Maybe she doesn't even know."

Jane sat feverishly in her hospital room. The white walls of the hospital were beginning to get to her. She had been more fearfully afraid than anything when she was lost, but now a new fear crept over her, a stomach-lurching one. A feeling that made her more helpless than she could imagine. Diana was only a few floors away from her, but she felt engulfed with panic. She relived the past few moments in her head.

Becky running into her room, gasping for breath and waving Jane's jacket about, saying how she had instructions from the doctor to give it to her. Jane frantically searching the pockets until she pulled out the beaten picture. Overcome with relief, smiling a rare smile, then Becky saying that Diana was in trouble. How she wasn't recovering well and she had to undergo another operation. Becky informing her that she had received word that her parents had been called and they knew that she was all right. Mixing all of the feelings that Jane could possibly have and sending them on a roller coaster through her heart. By the end of the confrontation, Jane didn't know what to think; she felt like she needed five minutes of plain silence.

Long hours pressed on and Jane lay there, staring at her situation. She prayed that in the end, Diana would be okay. She couldn't make it without her, without someone else to call upon every once and awhile to make sure that this happened this way. Without Diana, she was all alone. Without Diana, she was the only one who knew.

"Jane, how are you feeling tonight?"

"I'm not sure," Jane answered Doctor Walters.

"I want you to listen carefully. Diana isn't doing so well and she needs to stay in intensive care. But you, you are doing much better than her. We can walk and talk and all this stuff that Diana can't. I talked to your parents and they can't believe it, they are dying to see you. I don't know the whole story on you, but I know that you need your family. You may want to stay with your friend, but I think she would rather have you to go back to your home. Plus, it is your parents' decision since you are not an adult."

"You're going to send me home?"

"Yes, I'm afraid I must."

"What about Diana?"

"She will have to stay here; she's in no condition to fly on a plane."

Jane glanced at her withered jacket and then at the picture she held in her hand. As she took a closer look at the torn and beaten picture, a new burning fear began to surface in Jane's eyes.

The doctor continued to speak, "You're of no use to your friend here. Becky Lind, that lady that found you two, she's going to stay. She'll watch her."

Jane knew that the doctor really wanted her to go, and she wanted to return to her home more than anything! More than everything.

"I suppose just as long as you promise not to let her die and leave me."

"I will try my very best."

Jane looked at the doctor and just wondered if that would be good enough.

There is nothing to say about this. It wasn't meant to be this
way. When you tamper with fate, it never forgives.

Chapter 24

As soon as Jane had returned home, the press engulfed her, all wanting to question her. Jane told her parents to take her to the courthouse because it couldn't wait any longer. And that is exactly what they did.

Low clouds filled the sky, and small droplets touched the earth softly. It was a busy day even though it seemed alone. The trees stood firmly ready to take on the rain and whatever may follow. Beneath the entire hubbub stood the silence, even firmer than the rooted trees.

Jane sat in the car that had brought her, her mom and dad to the courthouse. Her parents tried to convince Jane to stay home and let them take care of the matter at hand, but after everything Jane had been through, she felt that this was her job, hers and hers alone. As the car pulled to a stop, Jane carefully exited. She winced slightly as her bandaged stomach turned sideways. Once she was standing up, she stopped and stared. The courthouse lay in front of her. Jane's mind flashed back and an eerie déjà vu feeling rushed through her head that made her want to turn and flee. But this time something was different; she wasn't standing here with Diana, unsure. She stood surrounded by press and police and that made her feel a newfound security. The rest of that day was a blur, a non-stop action that usually only happens...never.

Jane entered the courthouse. She opened the door slowly and was prepared to speak loud and clear. The only thing that kept her from being scared away was the thought of how this was her chance. This was what everything was for. Entering the courthouse, she was allowed into the courtroom. When Jane first walked in, she stared at the backs of Tom and Joe, and then at Sam Norman, who sat still in the defendant's chair. Without waiting to see if she was allowed to speak, Jane began to give a speech. She had to because handing in the picture wasn't going to be enough anymore.

"I have something of interest. I have been in an unusual nightmare. I say that it's unusual because I could not wake up from it. I came across a picture that proves the prosecutors an odd thing: guilty. Guilty of destruction of evidence to cover a crime, a murder that they helped commit. This picture is the same as the one handed in, except for the date. Let's start from the beginning..." Jane kept talking, much to the horror of Tom and Joe. They sat staring. They had heard about the two girls being found, but they didn't think that they could still hurt them, that after all this time they still held the picture. Tom was not as nervous because in his mind the picture only proved that someone had changed the date. It couldn't completely destroy them. "Maybe it could hurt our case against Sam, but who cares?" Tom sat back, a bit more calm.

Jane finished by saying something that made Tom sit up straight with a look of relief. She said, "And after all that! After almost dying! I find that my worn picture is not intact. You can just tell that it's the same, but it's all torn apart. The date is gone and in the wilds of the Amazon now."

The picture was handed in, and then Jane noticed Leea sitting in the back of the room. She smiled slightly and tried to mouth something to Jane, but Jane couldn't fully understand. All she understood was, "Hi...I've got something.........I've waited...I...scared."

Tom Hankar stood up and gave a speech on how this girl had been misinformed. Jane could tell that he wasn't his usual confident and clear self. Tom was trying his best, but the plane and every little thing didn't quite fit. Still, he knew that if he chose his words carefully, not all would be lost.

"In conclusion, she has found something important that I have yet to see. After test results, we will try to piece together who actually made a copy of the picture and why."

"I don't think that will be necessary, mister." A small voice could be detected from the back of the room.

"And why would that be, whoever just said that?" Tom answered slowly, slightly rocking back and forth on his heels.

Leea stood up and walked toward Barry Lonad, who was standing by the door of the courtroom. "These two gentlemen stayed at my house as you know," she said softly to him. "I felt sick inside when I realized who they were. I felt this way 'cause my friend Jane had called me and told me all about them before she left on her trip." Leea paused for a moment to stare at Tom and Joe. They shifted uneasily. "Anyway, that night that they were at my house, they confessed everything to me and..."

"Your honor, this girl has no basis and right to talk with Mr. Lonad. We are in the middle of a trail. She's not even under oath." Tom turned and stated.

"Let's just see what she has to say. It couldn't be any crazier than what the other one said."

Jane felt like someone had just thrown her down an endless hole.

Barry Lonad said softly to Leea, "I know that when you heard Jane was coming, you wanted to wait for her to tell me whatever it is that you wanted to say. Now that she is here, you can talk just to me. You don't have to talk to the whole courtroom."

"No, I want everyone to hear," Leea answered, then continued to speak, staring directly at Tom and Joe. "I thought that no one would believe the truth, because it's so crazy...sad and crazy and anything else. I racked my brain to make sure that I wouldn't have to live with the unbelievable truth my whole life. Here, this for you." Leea handed an object to Barry Lonad. Barry looked at it for a moment, then looked back at Leea. She nodded, and he pressed a button that was located on the side of it.

"What are you doing here? The question is, what are you doing here? Your mom invited us to stay. That's not what she meant, you idiot. Well, what then? I want to know what you did with Jane." Barry stared at the tape recorder as it kept on going, slightly broken up, but clear to anyone who was in that courtroom that moment.

Suddenly, something snapped inside Tom. He couldn't completely understand how this had started. Knowing now that all was lost killed him. An anger arose unlike any other, a strong, fearful anger.

"To know that getting on that plane, walking through a desert and everything else was so someone *else* could turn us in! I mean, think about it, Joe! Instead of that girl trying to get us with that picture we go through all this, kidnapping, assaulting and more, so someone else could turn us in! The irony in all of this! Now, it's even worse because a picture isn't much to contend with." Tom stopped for a moment to stare at Jane, his red fury growing inside him. "But a tape recorder! We not only risked our lives, we made them worse!"

He started running toward Jane and Leea. It was as if his steps were weighed into a slow motion picture that swept over the entire scene. Both girls turned and flew out of the courtroom, banging the doors behind them. The wet rain hit their faces as their feet pounded the sidewalk. Tom pushed through the press as they ran, and right as Jane's mom stepped outside of the building, it happened.

A high whistling noise pierced the silent air, cutting through everything like a steel whistle that whipped through the clouded atmosphere. She fell to the ground with thick, unwilling blood pouring steadily from her neck. The clouds from high above let small droplets of rain fall onto her limp body. Her sweet smile disappeared and her eyes misted over with a faint gray. She lay on the cold cement sidewalk with no more words left inside her and her eyes with their new dull appearance finally closing. Silence took over once again, a chilling, heart-stopping, dead silence that was broken by Mrs. McTerm's cry.

Which girl had it been? At first all were uncertain, even Tom, who dropped the gun and stood rooted to the spot.

It ended.

Everything settled, like the dust on a dirt road. It all came together somehow. Like a spinning top, it all has to give up and end somewhere.

Chapter 25

Tom stared blankly up at the small patch of light that came flooding through his cell. Staring into the empty space between him and the cell window, staring at nothing.

"Nothing," he mumbled. Tom was on death row. Joe was in jail for life in his mind. It was actually something like two hundred and fifteen years, but what did that matter? Sam was sentenced to life in prison but might get out. Might.

"Then he'll come and see me I bet," Tom whispered to himself as he toyed with a pebble. "He'll probably say how he would have done a much better job. How I must be the daftest person in the world to let things get out of hand, *that* out of hand. He must think that I'm so dense and ignorant." Tom sighed and flicked the pebble away, looking back up at the small window. "He won't get it. There was something else that tore things apart. He'll never understand because he doesn't know. He just doesn't know."

The same warm sun brightened the land, trying to lighten the mood. A light breeze stirred the air. Small colored birds sat on the thin branches of tiny trees. A few clouds lay still on the colorless blue sky. Everything was a light spring color, except for the black. The black moved through the lightness and brought it down, telling the birds to hush and the sky to scowl. The shiny black cars pulled into the cemetery just as the sun was beginning its decent. The cars were outdone by the number of people in black clothes, adding to the dampening mood of the day.

Everyone was there: family, friends, Heather and her mom, Barry Lonad and some other police men, Diana and even Leea with her mom. They watched the coffin with sad eyes as the priest began his speech. But all was lost on Heather, who still stood puzzled. She began speaking softly to herself trying hard not to cry out, "You were everything to me, Jane. You were my greatest friend. I don't know if I've brought this onto you. I hope with all my heart that I didn't. But just in case, I'm sorry. I'm sorry, Jane."

The funeral went on, and all stayed in a silent shock, hoping that this was a morbid dream. As they began to lower the coffin into the ground, each person in turn realized that it was a reality. After they had finished and the headstone was in place, one by one they began to lay flowers on the freshly dug dirt.

First, the policemen came and laid down one red rose each and then the most distant friends. Secondly, the slightly closer friends and the friends that had appeared after they came into money. Each one put down a bright red rose and said his or her regrets. All Jane's friends were there, including Whitney R. and Whitney B.; Lindsey; her bright blues eyes misted; Kaitlyn; Tanya; Ashley; Jen, and on and on. Then, the family began to walk by. It was the saddest sight they had ever witnessed. Tissues in hand, they tried to turn away but couldn't. After about half an hour, eleven people still stood: Mr. and Mrs. McTerm, Mark and Mike, Leea and Heather with their moms, Diana with her parents and family. The pile of bright red roses stared back at them, unwilling to be any help.

They stood as silence prevailed. No one spoke. Everyone thinking on how this could have even happened. Which turned into more complex thoughts and then to a silent goodbye that brought on a fresh wave of tears.

Finally, Leea spoke, and she spoke for all of them in the bravest way she could: "Jane was so courageous; we all loved her, and I don't think she'd want us to be mournful. She needs us to never forget. Jane knows that she did a great thing and that her life was not in vain. If Jane were able to talk with us right now, I think that she would want to say something heartbreaking but true." Remembering a favorite French saying she and Jane used to have, Leea swallowed, then finished rather shakily, "*C'est la vie.*"

Everyone looked at Leea, even the ones that didn't understand. Something in the way she had said it gave them enough strength to turn away, at least for the moment.

Mark turned to Mike, his eyes red. "You now, she never did get you back."

Mike smiled at Mark as he remembered his antics. "She would've gotten me back bad."

As they approached their cars Heather felt a chill fall down her back. An icy wind swept past her. As the breeze rushed through, she thought only one thought. A feeling crept inside her. Something she knew too well. "I have to let go," she thought. She needed to forget about it; it was over now. She wondered why she would get this feeling now. Pushing herself closer to her mom's car, she couldn't shake the feeling. It grasped her, whirled her around, and suddenly, she gasped. Her heart, never before more startled, seemed to pause and refuse to go on. Her eyes unwilling to take it in, her mind unwilling to understand. An unknown consternation crept inside her, and her eyes seemed to sharpen with careful precaution, not wanting to mislead her.

But they couldn't, because there it was, the unexplainable answer that somehow would always fit in her mind. On top of the pile of rich red roses laid the bright, resplendent, perfect, white rose, glinting back at her.

I'm sorry, Heather, for changing a life without the thought of any consequences, but I shall never know where my path ended and yours started. Remembering this story, I tried to teach you all I could so that not all would be lost. With each event I spoke to you, I know you heard me. And like I promised, I will always be in your mind. Whenever you close your eyes,

I'll be there, even if it's only a memory. What puzzled me was your effort in solving my help. I've grown rather soft on you lately so I've decided to tell. Heather, you did know, it was in that poem. I didn't lie. As you'll see I was just trying to help you. I suppose you don't care now, but I'll tell you anyway. The poem itself should have warned you enough, but in case it didn't, I even told you who else was in on the crime. First three lines, first letter in each line, it spelled it out perfectly, perfectly. I gave you the root of the problem, the essence. It all fit, even though, as I now realize, sometimes we never see the whole story, it wraps itself around us and blinds us, but see, Heather, you knew everything all along.

Printed in the United States
5471